Issam Ghazzawi is a Professor of Management at the University of La Verne. He received his Ph.D. from The University of Pittsburgh, his Master's in Labor and Human Resources (M.L.H.R.) from The Ohio State University, and his Master's in Business Administration (MBA) from Sul Ross State University. Additionally, he has more than 20 years of executive management and served on several organizations' advisory boards.

Over the years, he received numerous national and international academic awards. He also received numerous community, State of California Assembly, State of California Senate, United States Congress, and the United States Senate awards and recognitions for his service to the community.

He serves on the editorial review board of several academic journals. He started publishing children's stories in a foreign language at the age of 17.

For Serena and Ramsey Ghazzawi

Issam Ghazzawi

DANILO AND THE CHOCOLATE HILLS – BOOK 2

The Search for Carlo

Illustrations by Firas Al-Helli

AUSTIN MACAULEY PUBLISHERS™

LONDON * CAMBRIDGE * NEW YORK * SHARJAH

Ordering Information
Quantity sales: Special discounts are available on quantity purchases by corporations, associations, and others. For details, contact the publisher at the address below.

Publisher's Cataloging-in-Publication data
Ghazzawi, Issam
Danilo and the Chocolate Hills – Book 2

ISBN 9798886930771 (Paperback)
ISBN 9798886930788 (ePub e-book)

Library of Congress Control Number: 2021917581

www.austinmacauley.com/us

First Published 2023
Austin Macauley Publishers LLC
40 Wall Street, 33rd Floor, Suite 3302
New York, NY 10005
USA

mail-usa@austinmacauley.com
+1 (646) 5125767

20230802

Table of Contents

This storybook is a work of fiction. Although places of the novel are actual, names, characters, places, time, and incidents either are the product of the author's imagination or used fictitiously by the author. Any resemblances to actual persons, living or dead, names, events, or locales are entirely coincidental.

Dear Reader

If you have not read anything about Danilo and the Chocolate Hills, then before you read even one more sentence, you should know this: Danilo is a good boy, however his decision to skip school and go along with his good friend Carlo to the Chocolate Hills on the island of Bohol sets off a dramatic saga when the Evil Giant of the Hills turned them both into tarsiers. 'Tarsiers are small insectivorous, tree-dwelling, nocturnal primates with very large eyes, a long-tufted tail, and very long hind limbs.

From the first book of this series, we have learned that almost two months later, a monkey was able to only save Danilo from the Evil Giant and move him away from the hills into her colony, and was able to purify him through moonlight bathing at the seaside. When he got to be a boy again, he was able to go back to his family on the back of a dolphin's friend named Paco.

Day after day, Carlo's family and friends searched everywhere in and around the Hills, trying to locate Carlo. The sad news is Carlo was nowhere to be found. However, Danilo was determined to find and save his good friend Carlo from the Evil Giant of the Chocolate Hills.

This second storybook of the series *Danilo and the Chocolate Hills* will continue to take you through unusual situations, adventures, and unexpected incidents that young Danilo and his unexpected friends-a dolphin and a monkey will face in their uncommon plea to save Carlo from the Evil Giant of the Chocolate Hills.

With all due respect,

Issam A. Ghazzawi

Chapter One

It was around 4:30 AM on Saturday. The roosters were crowing when Cora and Ernie were just getting up to welcome a new day. Today is a special day, yet another beautiful, sunny day. Neither Ernie nor Cora was going to work, they wanted to spend the whole weekend with their son, Danilo.

As I shared with you in the first book of this series, Ernie, Danilo's father, is a fisherman who sets out in the middle of the night or in the very early morning to catch whatever fish he can with fishing nets that he had made and sell the catch in the nearby market with the help of his wife, Cora. He only owned a simple wooden fishing boat that he built with the help of his father and brothers which took them about three weeks to finish.

Danilo was quiet. He was staring outside the window, watching the chickens and the roosters running everywhere outside as they look for food. He can see one of the hens finding some food and then calling using her short, high-pitched, 'tuck-tuck-tuck!' it wanted her chicks to come over for food. Quickly, her chicks gathered around her and started eating, some newly born chicks were fed by her. This scene brought a little peace of mind to Danilo, he had never paid attention before to this. Danilo was amazed at how the hen was teaching her chicks how to eat, drink, and scratch for food. Every chicken playfully jumps around everywhere! The few roosters there were also cheerfully playing around with each other! It seemed like everyone inside and outside the house was happy, except for Danilo. He misses his friend Carlo, he is concerned about him being safe and is worried about him living his life as a tarsier in the Chocolate Hills.

In the meantime, Danilo's mom was busy cleaning the house and his dad was getting some eggs as he was tending to his chicken and doing some cleaning outside their little house.

When she was done cleaning the little house, "We want to celebrate your return by taking you to the Pahinungod festival that started last week," Cora said. "What do you think? This weekend is the festival's finale," she added as his dad sighed with relief.

"I don't feel like going anywhere," answered Danilo, his lips turned downwards. "I need to do something as I want Carlo to come back safe!" he asserted, his almond-shaped dark eyes staring out with such intense sadness.

His mom took a deep breath, knowing that it was probably just as likely that he'd change his mind later on and agree to go out with them.

Danilo looked tired, he was up late and did not sleep well. Confused if what had happened was true or a nightmare, he was imagining his life being a tarsier rather than a boy. That thought is what kept him crying. His parents were paying attention to him all night long. They tried to calm him down and help him sleep. Instead, he'd spent a few hours staring outside the window at the dark neighbor's home until he'd finally, seemed to drift off to sleep. He did not sleep much though. The nightmare of the Chocolate Hills and the loss of Carlo is what kept him up most of the night! He could still hear Carlo's voice asking for help. He was imagining himself still being a tarsier with huge eyes fixed in his skull, large mobile membranous ears, a long narrow tail, clinging vertically to a tree, leaping from branch to branch, jumping from tree to tree, and sleeping in the dark hollow close to the ground.

Just to remind you, the Chocolate Hills of Bohol Island in the Philippines, is about 1,268 hills that are mysterious geological formation; they are perfectly shaped and scattered in an area of 50 square kilometers, about 19 square miles, on the island towns of Carmen, Batuan, and Sagbayan. These mysterious hills have always been perplexing to many people. The unexplained existence of these hills baffled everyone's mind as to how they were formed.

He was never sure as to what exactly happened, but he remembered the night when they attempted to sleep on the coconut farm and the shrill alarming noise that came and interrupted the rumbling sounds of the thunder; and their encountering of the huge monkey with a long-tailed and a reddish-brown coat who breathe on them. He could also remember himself running up toward the Hills along with Carlo in the early morning and being surrounded by hundreds of chirping tarsiers hopping on the ground like frogs. He still remembered the changes going through Carlo's body and face while noticing and feeling the changes in himself too. Afterward, he can only remember him being in the monkeys' colony and realizing that the big monkey they met on the coconut farm was indeed the Mother Monkey who saved him from the Evil Giant of the Hills. Finally, he can still remember the day when he was walking by the seashore in the early morning and heard the strange sounds, "clicks, trills, chirps, whistles, and clacks," coming from the water and realized it was coming from his dolphin's friend, Paco, who was happily spinning in the air when he saw him. It was Paco who brought him back to his family in Calape (Calape is a relatively flat town on the big island of Bohol with sparse vegetation. What makes it unique is its crystal, clear water).

Suddenly, Danilo grabbed onto his mother's leg and screamed, "Hold me, Mom! Hold me, Mom!" Then his mom came closer and hugged him. Somehow, his parents managed to wipe their tears with their palms as they held their son.

"I want to bring Carlo back. I have to…I have to…I can't eat or sleep if Carlo is still away!" he was crying so hard he could barely breathe.

"I could have been hunted by someone or eaten by a feral cat that could be banished from nearby communities, or fall prey to a large bird, an owl, or a small carnivore," he continued saying as his imagination went too far. He was imagining him being in the Hills and living his scary life as a tarsier. He was wondering what might have happened to Carlo.

While talking, Danilo's eyes were red, and his pupils became huge. His parents were getting very emotional just by watching and listening to him.

"If Mother Monkey didn't come to save me, I could have been taken out as a pet or been displayed somewhere on the island by people and sold for trade."

"Daddy?" he asked. "Can you help me get Carlo back? We need to save him before it gets too late," an emotional Danilo pled and continued talking while sobbing and heavily breathing.

"I will, Danilo," his dad answered. "We must help bring him back. Let's discuss how I can help after you eat," his dad replied.

Minutes later, Danilo was sitting at the table and wanted to discuss getting Carlo back.

"I cannot eat, sleep, or function; Carlo is waiting for me to help him. I feel that I had betrayed him by being here alone!" While in tears, Danilo kept talking as his parents were listening and in tears.

"Is he going to make it safe?" Danilo cried out. "I need to talk to his family. I need to discuss this and give them more details so we can get him back. Please tell me he's going to be okay!" Danilo begged his parents.

"The best way to bring him is to go back to Mother Monkey and ask for her help. Um…" He sighed and then said, "Let's try talking her into bringing him, she is a good being, and I am sure she will help us," a heartbroken Danilo continued talking while his mom was a little buzzed by the whole conversation.

"I will be glad to go along. Do you know where Mother Monkey is?" his dad asked.

"No, I do not! I will ask Paco to take us there. I believe he knows how to take us to the shore where he brought me from. I know exactly how to get to the colony from the shore. Let's go to the Banana shore 'Danilo referred to this particular seaside as the Banana Shore, as this area of the seashore is a little curved, it looks like a banana' and sees Paco this afternoon, he knows that I will go there today," Danilo proposed.

"Very well, let's do that, Son!" his dad agreed.

"Can I go very quickly now to tell Carlo's family about our plan?" Danilo asked.

"While it is very early in the morning, we will go along and talk to them," his dad said.

Then in a few minutes, Danilo and his parents were on their way to Carlo's family.

It was a little after 6:00 AM when they arrived and knocked on the door of Carlo's family home. Quickly Carlo's dad, Andre, opened the door and urged them to get inside, and soon they were surrounded by Carlo's mom, grandparents, and siblings who got up and sat on the floor to listen to Danilo and his parents. Everyone was anxious to know more and see what they need to do to bring Carlo back. Carlo's grandma covered her mouth using both hands, trying to hold back her shrill screaming. She doesn't want anyone to hear her high-pitched cries. Carlo's grandpa was so quiet, trying to calm down his wife as he seemed demoralized.

On the other hand, while Carlo's dad seemed calm, his mom was far too distressed, her hands folded behind her head. She would linger outside the room for as little as she could to calm herself down before returning to listen. Pain welled inside her, an endless surging, though she still had not fully returned to herself and was unsettled. Carlo's siblings sat in silence, yet in tears wanting to listen.

"Thank you for coming to talk to us, I've just been up all night waiting to talk to you," Andre told Danilo.

Danilo looked stricken. He sighed. "Um, sorry…" His face was crimson (a phrase that means, a rich, deep-red color inclining to purple).

He turned his face toward the window and stared at the rainbow eucalyptus tree outside the house and said, "Um…I want to tell you exactly what happened!" Seems like he was so embarrassed to face Carlo's family and look them in the eyes.

Afterward, he started talking and provided Carlo's family with more details about the trip to the Chocolate Hills from the time they left their town of Calape, to the time they entered the Hills, the feelings of their transformation into tarsiers, and the changes in their bodies.

"I do not recall or knew what happened afterward," Danilo asserted. "I only remember living in the monkeys' colony." He also discussed in more detail their encounter with Mother Monkey and her role in his escape from the Hills and discussed the role of the dolphin, Paco, in getting him back to Calape.

Danilo's voice quavered at the end of his story. The thoughts of what he went through made it difficult for him to go through telling without thinking of his ordeal or what Carlo is currently going through.

"We will need to go and talk to Paco (the dolphin) this afternoon to seek his help in going back to the monkeys' colony, he knows the shore where he got me from. Mother Monkey is our only hope! I do not know where she is located on the Island, Paco does," Danilo stated.

Carlo's desperate family welcomed the news as a good plan to follow and agreed to go along with Danilo and his parents to the nearby seaside shore in the afternoon where Paco usually meets Danilo.

"Um…Um…I am so sorry, *tiyo* (a phrase to mean 'Uncle' in the local language) and *tiya* (a phrase to mean auntie in the local language)." A moment later, Danilo added, "I am not happy about what has happened and what we have done," with red, torn eyes and big pupils, crying guilt-ridden Danilo told Carlo's family. Besides, he was preoccupied with thinking of the right words and phrases to ease Carlo's family's pain and worries. Danilo wept.

"Will you forgive Carlo for going to the Hills without asking for your permission? Will you forgive me for going along with him? Can you forgive us?"

Andre folded his hands. It was hard for him to see Danilo's sad face. He took a deep breath then hugged Danilo and said, "Yes, I do forgive both of you. What a blessing you are, Son!" said Andre, "Think what we need to do now, let's work together, *kanyang* (to mean 'son' in the local language) and bring him back. Please remember that we love you the way we love our son. Carlo loves you very much, you know!" Andre said, he could tell from Danilo's voice that he was crying. Andre's voice broke completely.

"Thank you for being such a wonderful boy and a loyal friend to my son!" Andre said and then added, "You understand what I meant! Let's hurry up, help bring him back, and let's celebrate his return together." After these words, he embraced Danilo, who was attempting to leave but got as many tears as he had when he arrived at their home.

Carlo's mom nodded, feeling bad for Danilo, who looked sad and suffered a lot. He glanced briefly at her then stared again at the window.

"Okay, see you then this afternoon at the shore to the north of the town," Ernie said as the two families agreed to meet at 3:00 PM at the nearby Banana Shore where Danilo would meet Paco to explain the plan and ask for his help in locating the area where monkeys live.

To Danilo's relief, his dad poked him. "Then, let's go, Son," he whispered over Danilo's head while putting his arm over his shoulder and leading him out the door.

Danilo and his parents left Carlo's family home and took the short seaside route back to their home. They walked by the water unfazed by the waves that bring along seabirds and seals. On their way back, Danilo was still in tears and thinking about what the future hides. As he was staring at how the water was climbing up a long and striking at the seashore, it helped him hide the sound of his cry.

"I have a feeling I will be seeing Carlo soon," Danilo calmly told his dad.

His dad rubbed his shoulder and responded, "I am confident of his return! He will be back before you know it," he said. "I promise you my dear and look forward to seeing you both playing and going back to school together."

On their way, some kids were hanging out beside their home. A boy shouted as he approached Danilo,

"Wow…Wow…Wow! Is that you, Danilo? Happy to see you again! I see you are still alive! I am very surprised, they told us you had died!"

Danilo stood unmoving, but there was an avalanche going through his head; a sudden occurrence of bad memories and thoughts. He then tried moving his head as little as possible. But instead of answering back, he pressed his hands to his eyes, waited for the tears to dry, and then continued walking. Quickly, his dad told the boy, "Danilo is okay, he is just a little tired. Take care, Son; the story is not true!"

"Sorry, Uncle! I am happy that he is alive!" responded the boy then walked away with the other kids.

"Don't let it affect you, Son. Be strong! You know we love you," his dad affirmed, and his mom wrapped her arm around his shoulders as started sniveling (a phrase, which here means soft crying, also prone to muttering and erratic breathing).

"Hold on, Son, and do not worry!" his mother said.

In a little while, they arrived home; Cora began preparing breakfast, and Danilo was helping his dad tend to their chickens and roosters.

Chapter Two

Being home with his family, gave Danilo a sense of safety and security. Upon arrival, he sat down quietly looking at the window of their little home. He was staring at nothing! He was preoccupied with the thoughts of his past ordeal and the absence of his good friend who was left behind in the Chocolate Hills. He was unsuccessfully trying to remember just anything or to figure out his past as a tarsier. He was only able to remember the fact that he left home, his adventure, and the details that took place on his reaching the Hills, what he observed when their body changed, and finally, living in the monkeys' colony, and returning home with Paco.

Shortly afterward, his mom shouted, "Breakfast is ready!" she already prepared her son's favorite breakfast, the *Bangusilog* (*Bangusilog* is short for the combination of *bangus* 'milkfish', *sinangag* 'fried rice' and *pritong itlog* 'fried egg' and salad to go with it).

Ernie gave the blessing and then all said, "Amen!" All of a sudden, "I am not hungry, Mom," Danilo said.

"Don't think of anything! You just sit down and eat something, Danilo," his mom instructed, as she was looking a little uncomfortable with his answer. "I will get you some milk too."

"No, thank you. You do not have to do that. I'm fine," he replied.

"You don't look fine to me. You will need to sit down and eat with us. I won't be happy if you continue making excuses," his mom responded while his dad nodded in agreement. Upon sitting down, she reached out and gave him a cup of milk and filled his plate with milkfish, fried egg, fried rice, and added salad on the side.

As he was trying to eat, he was struggling with the thoughts of how it feels to be left in the chocolate Hills and living there as a tarsier. Later as he was drinking his glass of milk, he asked, "Mom, what does it feel like when someone becomes an animal?"

"Forget about that, Son, please eat! It was just a bad adventure!" his mom responded.

Danilo was struggling with the incident he encountered with the boy who he ran into this morning while on their way back from Carlo's house. How can he easily forget what the boy had said, "Wow…Wow…Wow! Is that you Danilo? Happy to see you again! I see you are still alive! I am very surprised, they told us you had died!"

Danilo felt another wave of regret, but he did not know what to do.

Cora took a deep breath, then, "There's not a lot you can do about that," she said. "I don't want you to keep thinking that way, Son."

While eating, his mom suggested that they would go out to watch the festival and treat him to shaved ice cream and lunch out. There would be just enough time for them to do so before going to meet Paco in the afternoon.

"All right," his dad said. "Let's do that, going to the festival is a good idea!" he added.

When finished eating and getting ready to go out, his mom surprised him with a new colorful T-shirt that has the festival logo in the middle.

"Wear it, Son, it will look nice on you," she suggested.

"Okay," he said, suddenly brightening. "I'll go."

Danilo put on the new T-shirt and soon they all were on their way out to the festival. He brought with him his little backpack containing a swimming suit and a towel so he can spend some time in the water with Paco.

The street that led to the festival site was full of people. On their way, they walked past many small shops and peddlers selling different clothing and food items.

"Dad! Can I have five pesos (equivalent to ten cents)?" asked Danilo as his eyes were staring toward the shirtless beggar who was sitting on the sidewalk wielding a begging bowl and stretching out one of his hands.

Ernie quickly plunged his hand into his pocket, brought out a handful of change, and gave it to Danilo who dropped it in the begging bowl.

"I am very proud of you, Son!" said Ernie as his mom nodded and shed some tears.

Danilo looked tired and drifting as they walked down the main street. Anyone who knew Danilo would describe him as a kindhearted kid. Like most kids his age, he was too well-mannered to state that if anyone asks him for something, he would agree to do it if it was all possible.

After walking a few blocks, they arrived at the old San Vicente Ferrer square where the festivity will take place. The square roared with rage for it now was awake from its peaceful slumber. The place was full of people. The square was also full of street vendors selling all types of decorative items, souvenirs, festival shirts, helium-inflated balloons, candies, food items, fruits, ice cream, shaved ice cream, sodas, bottled water, boiled and grilled corns, fried bananas, coconuts, and many other items.

At 10:00 AM, everyone in attendance stood and placed their right palms over their chests, while those with hats removed them, and proudly sang the national anthem of the Philippines while a decorated marching band was playing the anthem in the middle of the square. All the eyes were on the mayor of Calape who was raising the flag while surrounded by city and police officials.

Right after singing the national anthem, the mayor of Calape took the microphone and welcomed everybody saying, "As I welcome you all to our town, I am happy to chair this wonderful annual festival. This ten-day event in May honors the opulent (mean ostentatiously rich and luxurious) ancestry and spiritual heritage of the Bohol province as well as serves as a homage to Saint Vicente Ferrer, the patron of Calape town."

Quickly afterward, the drums of the *Pahinungod* festival (the word *Pahinungod*, means to offer in the *Bisaya* language-a local language) started banging and sending their booming sounds to the cheers and applause from the thousands of locals and non-locals who were there. Many spectators came to watch this festival from various parts of the Island of Bohol and the nearby Islands of Cebu and Leyte in the Central Visayas region of the Philippines.

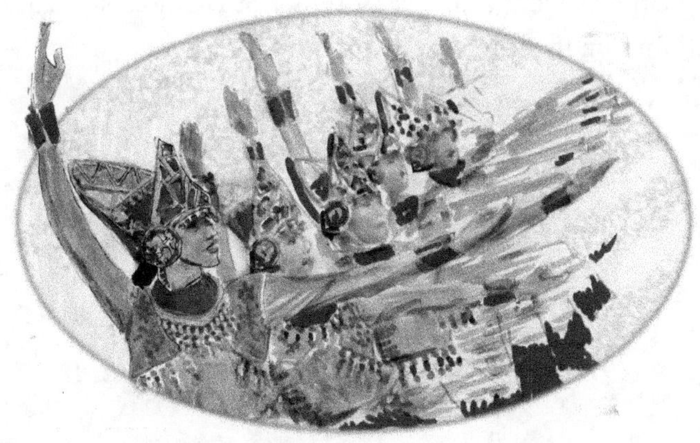

The bands and the dancers were dazzling spectacles of gorgeous handmade costumes. The lavishly decorated floats, meticulously choreographed dances, pulsating percussions, rhythm, beats, and of course, the music, and unique street traditional dancing steps left spectators amazed.

"Look at this beautiful float that is built on a truck and decorated with many different kinds of flowers. What beautiful costumes people are wearing while dancing on the float," his mom expressed as Danilo was quietly watching.

As the various marching bands and dancers were entertaining spectators, Danilo's parents were on the side cheering too. He was sitting calmly, apparently, his mind is somewhere else.

Suddenly, a big marching band that was led by eight flags' waving uniformed girls and followed by about 60 marching musicians dressed in colorful matching uniforms entered the square playing various musical instruments such as Cornet, Trumpet, Tuba, French horn, Clarinet, Flute, Oboe, Saxophones, Snare drums, Tenor drums, and bass drums. The band vibrated the cheering crowd.

This big band got Danilo's attention. Although the band had four bass drummers, Danilo could not stop staring at one of the drummers who was marching toward the last row of the marching band, wearing a nice decorated black and red jacket with an emblem of the festival, a black and a white liner matching hat, long black pants, white gloves, and white sports shoes. The bass drummer looked like a young 17- or 18-year-old boy with a contagious smile like Carlo.

Although older than Carlo, the drummer has dark brown skin, a rounded face, black hair, wide brown eyes, a wide nose, an average height, and a large build; he has a similar look to Carlo.

The thunderous sound of the bass drum sent Danilo a special vibration or wake-up call for him to search for his friend Carlo.

At any time, the bass drummer beats on the drum, and Danilo could hear the booming sound coming to his head as if someone saying, "Save me, Danilo! Don't leave me with the tarsiers."

Danilo continued quietly watching as his eyes welled up with tears and tears raced down his cheeks. He could hold the heartbreak no longer; Danilo fell to the floor in a disheveled heap and poured out in a flood of uncontrollable tears.

"Don't want to be here!" he cried out. "Want to go and see Paco!" He said, his anxiety rising and the drum was beating in his ears, blocking out all other sounds. He was worried if they stay any longer, he would miss meeting his dolphin friend as time was of the essence.

"It is a little early, Son, it is almost noon and we have plenty of time before meeting Paco," his mom responded as his dad nodded.

"Let's go and eat first. How about taking you to the close by Jollibee?" his mom suggested. She was referring to a popular fast-food chain in the Philippines.

"A great idea, Cora!" his dad said. "Let's get him a shaved ice cream first, then we will walk out of here."

Danilo was still quiet but agreed to his dad's proposal and walked along with his parents toward a vendor selling shaved ice cream in a decorated cart shaded with a colorful umbrella. The vendor displayed 12 big bottles containing various kinds of syrups. Danilo was trying to decide on what to add to the shaved ice corn, he was staring at the various bottles of syrups to decide which is more delicious, seemed all very delicious to him. He starred at the coconut syrup bottle, then at the cotton candy syrup bottle, the cherry bottle, the blue raspberry, the grape, the green apple, the strawberry, the honeydew melon, the chocolate, the blackberry, the banana, and finally the guava syrup bottle. Decision! Decision! Decision! To him, it was a tough choice!

Finally, he settled on the cotton candy and the strawberry syrups. As licking the syrups of the shaved ice cream, Danilo thanked his parents and offered his apologies again for being a bad boy.

"Not at all, Son, you are a good boy. Let's enjoy our day, your friend Carlo will be back soon!" his dad sighed and said with confidence while Danilo tried to focus on his colorful shaved ice cream.

After almost a ten-minute walk, they arrived at Jollibee. The place was packed. There was not a single seat available.

"Let me order for all of us while you take a table as soon as it gets available," Ernie said.

"That will be good; I think Danilo likes their fried chicken," Cora said.

"This is great, I will order chicken for all of us," Ernie responded.

Like any other fast-food restaurant, the place was hullabaloo (a term that here means a loud with continued noise or mixture of noises). The place was decorated with a Jollibee fictional mascot, which is a character of a bee whose body has red and yellow stripes. He has big black eyes and wears a red blazer with a black bowtie, a white chef hat, and yellow shoes. His wings are white.

In less than fifteen minutes, a table overlooking the busy street became available, so they sat down and waited for Ernie to come.

Ernie was standing in one of the long waiting lines to order. People of all ages crowded the place and the ordering lines. In about twenty minutes or so, he was standing before the order taker who also functions as a cashier. In a few minutes, his order was ready. He walked carrying a tray full of food and drinks toward the table where his family sat.

Then, "Look what I have for you," Ernie said, grinning from ear to ear and holding a red plastic tray that has a bucket containing six pieces of *Chickenjoy* 'Fried chicken', a Spaghetti Family Pack, three Peach Mango Pies, and three sodas.

"Here's your favorite fried chicken, my dear son!" his dad said as he was attempting to sit down.

While eating, "Is it time to go and meet Paco?" Danilo asked.

"It is still too early; we will go as soon as we finish lunch regardless. It will take us less than fifteen minutes to get to the Banana Shore. We will be there early," Ernie answered while Cora was trying to talk Danilo into eating and finishing his lunch.

"How do you like *chickenjoy* and spaghetti?" his mom asked him.

"I like it very much, thank you, Mom and Dad," he responded.

"Is this spaghetti better than the one I make at home?" his mom asked while smiling.

"Not at all, it tastes different, but I like yours more!" Danilo answered.

"Good boy!" Mom said. "Good…good…good…you will always be a good boy; we will continue to love you dearly!"

"Today is a special day; I am going to get you *Halo-Halo* for dessert," his dad said. (*Halo-Halo*, in the local language, means something like mix-mix, also spelled *haluhalo*. A popular Filipino cold dessert that is a mixture of crushed ice evaporated milk, and other ingredients including, *ube* (a bright purple yam), sweetened beans, coconut strips, sago (edible starch which is obtained from a palm and is a staple food in parts of the tropics), *gulaman* (seaweed gelatin), *pinipig* rice (immature grains of glutinous rice pounded until flat before being toasted; it is commonly used as toppings in the Philippines', boiled root crops in cubes, fruit slices, flan, and topped with a scoop of ice cream).

"*Halo-Halo*, for Danilo? This is very nice, Ernie, this is our son's favorite," said Cora. Danilo and Cora horsed around while Ernie went to get the dessert. In ten minutes or so, Ernie came back with a family-size bowl of Halo-Halo covered with mango, vanilla, chocolate, and coconut ice cream.

"It looks delicious, thank you, Dad! Um…Um…I'm so sorry…I know I got both of you in trouble, I wasn't thinking right. Am sorry I shouldn't have done it and I know I can't do anything about it now. I promise I'll be a good boy," Danilo was talking in a wheezy sound (an adjective that here means a sound by someone who has difficulty breathing).

"You are a good boy, Danilo!" his mom answered quickly while his dad was attempting to say something then let Cora continue. "We can't change the past; we are looking forward to raising you in a good way, our dearest. We love you, Danilo!"

"I look for the day when we bring Carlo along to have lunch and *Halo-Halo* with us here," Ernie said.

"Me too! I assure you, Mom and Dad," replied Danilo, "that I will always obey you and be a good boy; but I must tell you once more, that I am resolved to save Carlo and get him back!" Danilo was repeating himself.

Danilo's parents listened carefully to what their son told them, his mom could not help bursting out into tears while kissing his hand. Similarly, his dad gave him the 'okay or all right' gesture, made by touching together his thumb and index finger in a circle while extending his other three fingers and holding his wife's hand with his other hand.

"Indeed, Son," replied his father, "me too! I cannot help telling you that I am too determined to do whatever it takes to bring Carlo safe to his family!"

As they finished eating their *Halo-Halo* dessert, Ernie stood up and said, "It is time to move and go to meet Paco!"

An excited Danilo quickly wiped his mouth with the napkin, stood up, and pushed back his chair. He moved fast in an animated way (a term that is synonymous with energetic or full of life). To him, time was so important. He was anxiously awaiting this most important meeting of his young life.

At ten after two in the afternoon, they crossed the busy street to catch a fifteen-minute decorated *Jeepney* (also pronounced *Dyipne, it is* the most popular means of public transportation in the Philippines) ride to the Banana Shore where they will be meeting Paco.

As they step onto the back of the Jeepney and choose a space on the long bench seat to sit, Ernie shouted the name of their destination to the driver to confirm. The *Jeepney*'s travel route was painted on the side of the *Jeepney* while the final destination was displayed on the windshield. As the *Jeepney* carries on to the next stop, Ernie took out fifteen pesos (equivalent to $0.62

i.e. '62 cents' in US currency) and passed it to the person directly adjacent to him in the direction of the driver and said, "This is for three people." The passenger then passed it hand-to-hand to another passenger until it reached the driver.

On their way, the opened windows and backdoor *Jeepney* bumped along the narrow, sometimes paved and at other times uneven dirt road toward the Banana Shore. It was so hot and crowded, and sweat poured down everyone as they all stayed still next to each other.

Danilo's parents were anxiously quiet and waiting to arrive at the Banana Shore, neither of them moved a muscle. Danilo could hear his heartbeat; he could only hear Carlo's plea for help.

Chapter Three

It was around 2:15 PM when they arrived at the seaside which Danilo calls the Banana Shore, Carlo's family was already there waiting.

"*Magandang hapon*!" (which means 'good afternoon' in the local language) Carlo's dad, Andre, greeted everyone.

"*Magandang hapon sa iyo masyadong*!" (it means 'good afternoon, to you too' in the local language)

Ernie and Cora had responded simultaneously and the two dads shook hands as the wives hugged each other. Carlo's dad and mom gave Danilo a big hug.

Happy to see you all! Andre, said while all eyes were on the seawater. All were quiet and awaiting the arrival of Paco, the dolphin. Andre was constantly playing with his hair and scratching his head. Carlo's mom, Sonia was a little withdrawn into herself, she tended to shut herself off, and zoned out. She looked a little less social and more nervous.

On the other hand, Danilo was quietly crying. It was so difficult for him to explain his feelings to anyone else. As no one can understand what he went through, no one had to deal with what he dealt with. Cora was very sympathetic and quiet, she was holding her son's hand and trying to calm him down. His dad was also quiet and seemed he was biting the inside of his cheeks. Everyone seemed anxious!

Shortly, a slapping sound of a body part against the surface of the water was accompanied by a splash everywhere. Paco just arrived! Paco was whistling in frequency as he spun happily into the air, he meant to say something like, "I am very happy to see you." Paco kept spinning and whistling, he wanted Danilo to come and swim with him.

In the meantime, Danilo, his parents, and Carlo's parents were waving and blowing kisses to happy Paco.

Quickly Danilo put on his swimming suit and took a dip in the water to swim with Paco.

In a little while, "Stop…Stop…Please stop! I need to talk to you!" Danilo shouted as he gestured with his hands for Paco to stop and listen.

After several gestures, Paco sensed Danilo's needs to talk. He cooled down and came very close to Danilo; he felt a surge of happiness. Paco's mouth touched Danilo's face; his beautiful friendly face and his big smile expressed his feelings, "I miss you, Danilo!" alternatively, as if he was also saying, "I can't believe, we are back together playing!"

"I need your help, Paco…We need to go to the same seashore you found me the other day when I was staying nearby in the monkeys' colony. We need to meet and talk to Mother Monkey," a distressed Danilo said.

"You are not going back to live there?" asked Paco.

"No! Not at all! I will never go back to live there again. I will only go there with my dad and Carlo's dad to talk to Mother Monkey to help us find Carlo. She is the only person who can help us…Um…Um…" responded Danilo while in tears.

Paco sensed Danilo's grief as he was patiently listening and asked, "But how would you all go there?"

"We need your help, Paco, to get us there. We will follow you in my dad's fishing boat. Do you remember how to get there?" Danilo asked.

Paco made some burst-pulsed sounds, (a term that means a rapid series of broadband clicks) shook his head, and went into a silent time for a few minutes. Danilo was in a state of confusion.

Suddenly, Paco slapped his fluke against the surface of the water and said, "I will take you there! But I will need to search the area again to be able to locate the place as I do not remember exactly. As you know, all shores look similar." Paco went back into a deep silence while seeming compassionate.

"I will go back and start searching the shores, I hope I will remember!" then Paco added, "I will slowly search and try to use whatever sense I have to find the monkeys' area. I am glad they came to say goodbye to you when I saw you there. I feel that I can sense them."

Danilo got relieved a little bit when hearing what Paco had just said. He gained a little hope.

"When can you start searching?" Danilo asked.

"I will start looking for the place immediately!" Paco answered.

"Okay…Okay…I will be waiting for you at this spot, my friend. You are the only one who can help us," Danilo stated.

Paco made a range of different sounds through his nasal air sacs and quickly started a forward-moving up and down as Danilo and others were watching his powerful muscles running along the backbone and the sides of his body move the tail up and down, providing the power that pushes him deeper into the seawater.

Like other dolphins, Paco's eyesight is incredibly acute; he has an eye on each side of his head, which gives him a panoramic visual range of 300 degrees. Each eye can move independently of the other, meaning he can look in two different directions at the same time. He can see behind himself too. Additionally, Paco and other dolphins have a reflective layer of cells just behind the retina called the '*tapetem lucidem*' (a term from the Latin language to mean *bright tapestry*. It is a layer of tissue in the eye of many vertebrates. It contributes to the superior night vision of some animals; this helps them to see exceptionally well in low light). A dolphin can also see just as well out of the water as well as in it.

In addition to his incredible eyesight, Paco is also capable of hearing frequencies at least several times higher than us human beings. His eyesight and hearing will be a big plus in mapping out the area and locating the monkeys' colony.

When Danilo told everyone what he discussed with Paco, they all got a little sense of relief and inspiration.

"I guess it took about two hours for Paco and myself to get back from the monkeys' colony the other day," Danilo said but wasn't sure.

"Two hours each way? That's not so bad, we can wait here," Cora said.

Everyone was quietly sitting on the soft and smooth sea-sand looking at the majestic deep blue sea with its waves lapping on the shore. They did not mind the brightness of the sun in their eyes or the high humidity that made the wait uncomfortable. However, the hope of seeing Carlo was more important than anything that bothered them. It seemed as if the breeze coming from the sea tides and the sounds of the waves helped to ease the waiting time while interrupting their silence. For them, the wait was endlessly coupled with desperation.

Danilo laid back on the sand and closed his eyes, trying to rest. He'd felt that the centerpiece of his historical adventure was dug up and exposed as an utter fiction story. It left a wide-open wound he couldn't quite overcome.

"Hey, Danilo, you sure needed that nap! Take a break and rest," his mom said.

While waiting for Paco's return, children on the seashore were playing all over the place, some were building sandcastles, others kicking the ball, and others covering their bodies with sand while keeping their faces out to grasp for fresh air and sea breeze. Some families gathered to socialize and enjoy early dinner. Birds and seagulls seemed to be friends there, they were funny as they were coming closer to people to get food or to steal some food. Danilo was eyeing in amazement the seagulls flying and the waves crashing against rocks.

Suddenly, "I'm frightened!" Carlo's mom, Sonia, cried.

"Please don't tell me we can't find Carlo!"

"Just relax, my dear; let's keep our faith that we are going to find him safe!" Andre said patiently in his low-pitched voice and hugged his wife while Danilo and his parents' faces looked wanly (a term to mean they were looking with a tired and sad expression on their faces).

The sun, now a fiery orb in the sky gradually receded into the water below. Everyone was impatiently waiting and looking at the waves hoping Paco will appear and bring some good news. The hours everyone spent waiting were bleeding together and no one knows what the passage of time brings, it just felt interminable (a term here to mean continuous).

In the meantime, Paco was on his mission to find the monkeys' colony. He swam all over the island, searching the seashores in the hope of finding the monkeys. Finding the right colony is not easy at all; all shores look alike. Very importantly, other than his intelligence, Paco does not use a map nor does he know anything about maps.

As he was searching the sea closer to the shores, Paco started producing a wide range of sounds in the air by releasing air through his blowholes. These sounds were something like *"seeessssscccch, scroooooooootch, scroooooooootch, vreeeeecccccch!"* he seemed that he was communicating with his pod. It also seemed that he wanted to say to his family something to mean, "Don't worry about me, I am helping Danilo. I will be coming to see you later."

Paco was busy searching the island; he was leaping from the waves as he was swimming alongside ships on the west side and the northern tip of Bohol Island. He stopped at various locations and at various times to look at the land from far away to see if he can hear the sound of the monkeys. His eyes were moving in different directions; Paco wanted to make sure he is in the right area; he knows that the monkeys are living close to the shore.

Suddenly, an unusual squeak started coming out from Paco, "*Sooooowooooooosh, Sooooowooooooosh, Sooooowooooooosh!*" he was in distress; apparently, something went very wrong! he started bleeding around his pectoral fin (flipper) and nose.

Paco continued his squeak and distress whistles. He came very close to the shore in the northern part of the Island, closer to the town of Inabanga. Crying for help, a couple of fishers and other people who happened to be there, rushed to see the distressed dolphin. They noticed that the dolphin's movements seemed unnatural. He made a few passes as they quickly noticed that a fishing line entangled his pectoral fin. They did not doubt that Paco came to the shore asking for help.

All were compassionate and sympathetic. Very quickly, a couple of fishers told the people around to assist them in helping the dolphin as they have some experience in doing so.

One man shouted, "Hey guys! Just follow our instructions! Let my buddy and I figure it out. Just hold the dolphin as we work on it, do not let him move his face."

"It is a delicate job, it requires experience; we cannot jeopardize his life. Again, please follow what I say!" the fisher added.

"Okay, we will do!" one bystander responded and others already started holding the dolphin and pulling him closer to the shore.

Quickly, one fisherman tried to cut and remove the fishing line with a small knife he usually carries to help him in cutting the fishing lines when needed while fishing. At the same time, the other fisher removed the fishing hook out from Paco's pectoral fin. What's unusual was the fact that Paco not only went to the people once for help but swam away in pain and went up for air and then returned for more aid. He was sure they are trying to help him. He continued squeaking and making distress whistles. He was saying something like,

"*Sooooowoooooosh, Sooooowoooooosh, Sooooowoooooosh!*" he meant to say, "Please help me… I am in severe pain!"

Everyone there understood these painful sounds and felt for the dolphin. They just didn't have the words to describe how they felt. They felt bonded with him and assured him through their compassionate work and look that they are there to help him pass through his suffering. Paco sensed that feeling!

While cutting the fishing line, one man was explaining to all by saying, "These lines can impede dolphin movement and impair foraging abilities, leading to starvation, systemic infections, and debilitation (meaning, making someone very weak) from severe tissue damage, pain and distress, and in some cases, death." Everyone was listening, showing support and compassion, and pledging a commitment to follow instructions.

It took everyone over an hour of work to untangle the fishing line and for the rescue team of random people who happened to be there to feel comfortable that he can survive. It was careful teamwork as any mistake could have led to the dolphin's death.

Afterward, Paco rested on the shore while still in pain. The people who were helping tried washing the blood away and drying the injury with whatever clothes they had on them. They were so sad to see him injured. Some were in tears, but no one knew how long he has been suffering.

After a little while, Paco swam off looking good enough but still weak, emitting sounds like whistles as he went on. He was saying something like, "Thank you very much for saving my life, I owe it to you forever! I will always be there to help you all when you need me!" Paco waved to everyone while in pain.

People were happy watching him swimming while waving back, hoping the salty water of the sea could help to heal him fast.

"Salamat (thanks) to you all! It was successful and collaborative work, much appreciated! The removal of the plastic line around the dolphin will allow the wound to heal," the older fisher said as he shook everyone's hand.

"*Walang anuman* (you are welcome), sir," everyone answered back.

A young man came closer and said, "I very much appreciated what we all have done…I am glad we had the experienced fishermen who led us on this incredible work!"

"*Kayong lahat ay gandang gabi sa* (a term to mean, 'you all have a nice evening') Bye!" the young man said and left.

Back in Calape, the blazing sun was moving through the white clouds, illuminating the sky in a bright orange color that was reflecting on the sand of the seashore. The sea breezes gently sway the coconut leaves as the clear night sky was moving in while the wave stops as it reaches the tide line and slowly rolls back into the churning seawater! (Churning seawater is a term to mean the water was moving about violently.)

The shore was also getting very quiet as most of the people and children already left. What interrupted the quiet evening was the sound of seagulls and waves crashing against the shore. As they stared at each other, Danilo, his parents, and Carlo's parents, became very worried. Paco has been gone for over five hours.

Noticing the worry of some people, Andre interrupted their silence and said:

"We have no choice, let's keep waiting. He is looking around to find the right location."

Andre's face must have shown his worries too. His wife quickly asked and in a soft, yet disturbed tone, "What's wrong?"

"Nothing wrong! I only meant that we will need to be patient a little, finding the right location takes time," Andre replied as his wife Sonia was pressing her lips together, Danilo was distracted, Cora was biting her lips, and Ernie nodded his head in agreement with Andre. They all had their version of anxiety.

"Um…Just keep waiting and I will be back shortly! I will get you some water and snacks from the nearby peddler," Ernie said.

"No need for this. I am not hungry nor thirsty; honestly I am not. I can wait. I just want to wait for some news." Sonia was still emotional and desperate.

"I will accompany you," Andre suggested. "Let's go, Andre!" Ernie said.

The two dads quickly walked away for less than ten minutes and brought back bottled water and potato chips for all.

As they impatiently sat and waited, a sudden squeak came from the water coupled with a splash. Paco just arrived and revived everyone's hope. Except, he was not spinning in the air or being as active as before this time. Danilo's blood was pounding in his ears (a phrase which means here that his heart was beating faster and his blood pressure was high)

Danilo rushed toward him. "Are you okay? What happened to you?" he quickly asked and started crying. Slid his eyes away, too frightened to see him injured. He was scared and shivering in the water, and felt his heartbreak.

"Sorry," he said. "I'm sorry to put you through this." He sobbed.

Paco responded with weak squeak sounds, he was saying, "I am okay…it is not your fault at all!"

When they realized that Paco was injured, all hurried toward him and were horrified. Ernie grabbed a bottle of water so quickly and washed the injured part as Andre was looking closely everywhere to make sure that no line was still there.

The scene was so emotional; everyone had a bit of guilt and anxiety. Watching what was going on, Danilo, Cora, and Sonia were weeping like babies. They were in total distress as they watched. They felt a sense of defeat. What makes it defeating was the fact that the future is so uncertain! It seemed to them that almost everything that can go wrong did go wrong!

"I will get him some help! Stay with him and I will be back as soon as I can," Ernie said and quickly left for the police station.

When getting to the police station, "*Magandang gabi ginoo*," (it means 'good evening, sir', in the local language) "I need your quick assistance in reaching out to someone who works for the Island's Marine Mammal and Fishery Center to help an injured dolphin."

"Okay, let me see what I can do," the officer responded and quickly started calling out. After a few calls and a few conversations, the officer hung up and said, "Please just wait for a little, someone will be here shortly."

After twenty minutes or so, a man quickly entered the police station, saluted everyone, and said, "Come with me to assist the dolphin, I have my car outside."

In less than fifteen minutes, they arrived there and the Marine Mammal and Fishery Center's doctor carrying a big white first aid box rushed to Paco and started examining him as all were watching. Very quickly, this doctor wiped out the injuries with disinfectant sprays, sewed the injured parts, washed them well to facilitate the recovery, then injected him with some vitamins that would revitalize his organism. As the doctor was sewing the injuries, Paco was enduring severe pain. You can see it and feel it through his face, eyes, and squeaks. He squirmed (a term to mean displaying discomfort or distress through twisting and turning his body around). Everyone was watching closely, yet no one spoke for at least forty-five minutes.

"I am done, he is good to go now! I wish him a speedy recovery!" the Marine Mammal and Fishery Center's doctor said. "Good night, everyone!" he added and left.

"Paco...Paco...Please don't die on me, I love you!" Danilo said. "Um...I am so sorry about what happened!" Danilo must have been more distracted than he realized because it took him some time to understand what was happening.

Paco shared a glance and a hint of a smile then said, "I will be back after two sunrises (he meant after two days). I think I will be okay then and will be able to figure out the monkeys' colony soon. I was in the area of the monkeys before I got injured." His eyes were cool and clear. He swam off the shore while showing off his affection and appreciation to everyone.

It was getting late that night; the two families headed home and agreed that they will go back to the shore after two days of 'two sunrises' to wait for Paco.

They rode a *Jeepney* to get back home. Upon arrival, Andre reminded them of an old saying, "At any given moment, you have the power to say this is not how the story is going to end."

"*Magandang gabi,*" (which means good night in the local language) everyone said.

Chapter Four

"At any given moment, you have the power to say: This is not how the story is going to end!" That was the last statement Andre said before saying good night the night before last. This message simply suggests confidence or assurance in the possibility that what one desires will be accomplished by not giving up. It also implies that hope is a good thing, maybe even the best of things, and good things never die.

Danilo stayed up all night thinking about Carlo and Paco, and about the time when he goes back to the monkeys' colony. It was so hard for him to sleep and simply forget about all of these challenges in his young life. His mind was working non-stop. He is missing Carlo. He also feels bad for what happened to his dolphin friend and wonders if Mother Monkey will agree to offer her help to save Carlo.

"I am afraid Paco is not well and will not show up again…I am afraid that if even he showed up, he cannot find the monkey's colony…I am also afraid even if we found the colony, Mother Monkey will not be able to help us. How about if she wants to help us and was not successful? Would she also get hurt?" Danilo was doing lots of self-talking. If you had looked into Danilo's sleeping pattern, you would have seen him crying all night long. He was not able to sleep until he could no longer keep his eyes open.

Early Tuesday morning and that would be the interpretation of Paco's last statement, "I will be back after two sunrises." Both families were ready to get back to the Banana Shore in hope of meeting Paco.

It was around 4:30 AM when the doorbell rang and Carlo's parents were outside waiting in the last stain of darkness for Danilo and his parents to go and meet Paco. Everyone was ready to start a new journey in their search for missing Carlo. Andre starred east to where the sun has just begun lifting its golden ray over the town. He knows that today's sunrise is a new chapter of his life. It might signal the beginning of what they hope will be a good end.

"Good morning, Brother Ernie, Sister Cora, and dear Danilo!" Andre said as Sonia greeted Danilo and his parents.

"Good morning to you too," Ernie and Cora responded.

"I hope today will be a good day," Ernie said.

"Let's keep our faith alive!" Andre responded and quickly they crossed the street to walk for about a few minutes to catch a *Jeepney*'s ride on their way to the Banana Shore to meet Paco.

The town was getting up at this early time of the day. They could have heard the honking horns of the *Jeepneys* on the main road, the chirping of the birds, the barking of the dogs, and the crowning of the roosters everywhere. By now, most of the daily peddlers have already started their day. Therefore, the search for the missing Carlo had begun with hope. They caught the *Jeepney* that was parked at the intersection of *Main Street* and *P. Ocampo Road,* then headed toward the Banana Shore.

Upon arrival, Paco was there waiting. He looked better, however, they all sensed he is still not feeling well. He was not as affectionate as he used to be, he was trying to smile and make everyone comfortable.

"I know you aren't feeling well but hopefully you will be better very soon!" Ernie told Paco while Danilo was hugging him in the water.

"I am okay and be ready to go along to the monkeys' colony today," Paco responded.

"This is great, thank you, Paco!" Danilo said, looked at his dad, and asked, "What is the plan?"

"Um…I will get my boat quickly…I guess we will also need to get some food and water. We also need to buy some fruits to give to the monkeys as a token of our appreciation," Ernie said and all agreed.

Ernie faced everyone and said, "Let's share responsibilities! I cannot fit everyone in the boat, I suggest that only Andre, Danilo, and I go to the monkeys' colony and moms wait at home. I also suggest that I also go and bring the boat closer to this shore, and then Andre and I go to the market to buy bananas and other fruits to give to the monkeys. I will also get some food and water for us as we have no clue how far and how long we will be going."

"Besides all of this, I will also need to have the Marine Mammal and Fishery Center's doctor checks Paco's injuries one more time. We owe it to Paco to ensure he is also well!" Ernie continued. "It will be a good idea that Danilo stays with Paco and wait for us here," Ernie added.

"It is a good plan, let's do it!" Andre suggested.

As Carlo's mom was so quiet, Sonia must have been more distracted than she ever realized, because it took her a few minutes to comprehend what Ernie had said. On a day this stressful, she could already guess things started going in the opposite direction.

Sonia's eyes opened wide with disbelief, "Are you serious? I can't go?"

As she said so, Ernie felt a shift and then said, "Sorry, Sonia and Cora, it will be easier as we have no room on the boat. Besides, it will be easier to manage this way. This is not a fun trip."

Sonia had wanted so badly to go to the colony but hadn't insisted that she goes, because there was no room on the boat. She stepped back and tried to hide her disappointment as tears were getting into her eyes. She looked at Ernie and Andre and told them, "Please be careful! Don't make us worry."

Cora nodded and added, "Please do! We cannot afford to be worried! We will anxiously be waiting for you all to come back."

"Shall we wait for you here?" Sonia asked.

"No…No! It is not a good idea, please go home and wait there," Andre responded. Sonia and Cora reached out and hugged everyone.

"Bye for now!" Cora said while walking away with Sonia. Both moms left, their tears welling from deep inside and coursing down their cheeks. They both unsuccessfully tried hard to hold back their tears.

While leaving, Cora and Danilo shared a glance, even a hint of a smile. Moments later, Danilo's face lit up. "Oh yes," he said. "I've always wanted to spend time with Paco, especially at the time of his illness. I will be taking care of him until you get back."

"How do you communicate with your family?" Danilo asked Paco.

"How do we communicate? We usually make two kinds of sounds, 'whistles' and 'clicks'. While we use clicks to sense our surroundings through echolocation, we use whistles to communicate with other dolphins, members of our pod, and in some instances with other species. Each dolphin has a unique whistle called a 'signature whistle', which is used to identify an individual," Paco answered.

It is important to note here that pod life plays a very important role in protecting dolphins from predators such as sharks. Very importantly, dolphins are social mammals that interact with one another. They too swim together, protect each other, and hunt for food as a team.

"Let me teach you how I communicate with my pod via a whistle," Paco told Danilo and started "*Pawooo...Pawooo...!* I am saying hi to them. Each of us communicates at a slightly different vocal pitch which allows us to understand which dolphin is speaking. My pod's family knows it is me when I say, '*Pawooo...Pawooo...!*'" said Paco.

"Let me try to say it," Danilo responded and started whistling, "*Piawooo...Piawooo!*"

"Not quite right! It is *Pawooo...Pawooo...!*" said Paco.

"Pawwoo, Pawwoo...!" repeated Danilo.

"A great job, Danilo! However, my vocal pitch is different from yours! Regardless, you are now a member of my pod and a dolphin brother!" Paco said jokingly while maintaining a big smile. They laughed aloud!

"Can you teach me how to greet someone?" Paco asked.

"It is easy, I say 'hi' or sometimes we say 'hello'," Danilo answered and asked Paco to say 'hi'.

"Hi...hello...hi...hello," Paco repeated and laughed. Danilo laughed aloud and hugged Paco.

As they were laughing, Ernie just arrived, he brought his blue single-engine boat to the Banana Shore, docked it there, and rushed with Andre to the nearby fruits and vegetable market as Danilo was keeping Paco company.

About an hour or so later, they returned from the market with a box of bananas, a box of watermelon, and a mixed fruit box containing coconut, oranges, and other fruits that the peddler had for sale at a discounted price. The fruits were their gift to the monkeys. Additionally, they got a cooler that contained food, snacks, and water for their use. Ernie also brought a tank that is full of fuel as he is afraid that the boat's fuel capacity might not be enough; no one knows where this journey leads or how many hours it might take.

The day was getting sunny with a gentle breeze and the race against time had started.

"Andre, please load everything while I will quickly go to the Marine Mammal and Fishery Center and bring the doctor to see Paco," Ernie said and quickly ran out to bring the doctor to check on Paco.

"What a brave and sincere boy you are, Danilo!" Andre murmured and started loading up the boat.

Bowing his head as the dark circles were apparent under Danilo's eyes as he was not able to sleep well for some time, responded with a shy smile, "Thank you, *tiyo* (which means 'Uncle' in the local language). I would like to assure you again that I am so sorry regarding what happened."

"It is meant to be, Danilo! There's no need to apologize, Son. Things will soon get better and my son will be back with all of us! Let's keep our hope alive!" Andre responded and continued loading the blue boat.

Paco on the other hand was displaying some energy. However, it was not at the same level as it used to be. It was apparent that he was still not feeling well. He tried to play with Danilo and spin a little bit; however, he was still weak.

"Forgive me, Paco! I should've listened to you and others before I went to the Chocolate Hills with Carlo," Danilo said.

"Do not worry now, it already happened! Can you tell me more about what happened?" Paco asked.

Danilo came closer to Paco and started telling him the story of what happened, Paco was carefully listening however, he was getting very confused; he has no clue what Danilo was saying or explaining. He did not respond, he just shook his head and sighed. Paco is not familiar at all with the complexity of the situation, his knowledge, and life experience is limited to the water; Paco has had no exposure outside the sea.

Meanwhile, it was around 8:30 AM at the Marine Mammal and Fishery Center when Ernie entered the center and greeted the woman and her associate at the reception desk, "*Magandang umaga kaibigan*! (he meant to say 'Good morning, friends', in their local language). I am looking for a doctor. Umm, I guess his name is Domingo, not sure!"

The young woman and man who worked there simultaneously answered him back by saying, "*Magandang umaga ginoo*!" (They meant to say 'Good morning, sir', in their local language.)

Then the young woman who appeared to be the supervisor said, "Yes, we have a doctor by the name of Domingo, he will be here soon, just give him a couple of minutes."

"Thank you, ma'am, I will wait," Ernie responded and took a seat there waiting. He knows that a couple of minutes could be 20 minutes, half an hour, or maybe an hour. He had no other choice but to wait.

While there, he was looking at the various posters of dolphins and other types of fish that seemed very familiar to him as a fisher. Then he picked the center's magazine and started reviewing some educational marine life articles relevant to sick and injured marine animals, and other marine research. Then, it was almost 20 minutes later when Domingo arrived, noticed Ernie, and greeted him by saying, "Good morning, friend, how can I assist you?"

"Oh! Good morning, Doctor Domingo, I am here to again ask for your help in checking the injury of the dolphin that you treated a few days ago," Ernie said.

"How does he look? I hope he is better now! Let me see," the doctor said and added, "Thank you, friend, for taking care of the injured dolphin, what you are doing compliments our mission of rescuing, rehabilitating, and releasing marine mammals who are injured, ill, or abandoned."

"Let's move quickly and see the injured dolphin. You will ride with me," said the doctor.

They both rushed to the center's small parking lot where the doctor's old white, full of dust tiny small car had been parked.

"Excuse the dust outside and the mess inside the car!" the doctor apologized and Ernie quickly responded with a big grin on his face, "Not a problem at all, Doctor…I even do not have one. No need to mention that dear doctor Domingo!"

Later on, and after a short drive, they arrived at the Banana shore.

Quickly the doctor moved closer to the dolphin into the water and sat near Paco who seemed to remember him.

"I see you're recovering well from the injury, my dear dolphin friend! How do you feel?" the doctor asked Paco.

"*Shrrisheee showoow*!" Paco shrieked, which probably meant something like "am okay, thank you!"

It took the doctor another twenty minutes to finish examining Paco and checking out the injuries. Then, he opened his medical bag, sanitized the injuries one more time, gave Paco some vitamins, and said as he was wiping the injuries with a medicated solution, "The vitamins that I gave you, will make you more comfortable and more energetic. I also suggest that you rest more, it'll help you."

"*Showoow*!" he meant to say thank you!

Paco then opened his eyes and showed the doctor a big smile. Quickly, an emotional dolphin moved inside the water, produced emitting sounds, spanned a little, and waved. He continued making some sounds and whistles that meant something like, "Thank you doctor for seeing me again and for saving my life. I very much appreciate what you are doing to me and other mammals!"

"Take care friend!" the doctor waved to Paco.

"Thank you very much, doctor! Is he okay now?" Danilo asked as Andre and Ernie were paying close attention.

"He is fine, he is recovering well. He needs more rest to fully recover," the doctor answered then stated, "You seem to be good friends."

"Yes, we are indeed good friends! He also taught me how to whistle to his pod," Danilo answered.

"Good job, boy! This whistle is your dolphin's friend's name. Every dolphin has a specific signature whistle," the doctor told Danilo. "They can remember the signature whistle of each other even after the separation of as much as 20 years. One important thing you should know is dolphins can transfer and receive information with several sound-producing organs 20 times more effectively of the amount than humans can through ears."

"Wow! This is amazing! I did not know that," answered a surprised Danilo.

"Take care," the doctor said and saluted everyone before leaving the shore to go back to the center.

As soon as the doctors left, "What would you suggest? Can we keep the plan or wait?" Andre paused his question to Ernie and Danilo with a pretended smile. He was crumbling inside. He cannot wait to see his missing son.

"I think Paco is okay and he can take us today. What do you think, Dad? Can we go now?" an emotional Danilo stated. His tears raced down his cheeks. He swiped at his eyes but the tears came anyway.

With a single drop of grief welled up from the corner of his eye, Ernie responded by saying, "Let's ask Paco one more time."

The three approached Paco who was smiling at them. Danilo came closer and asked him, "How do you feel, Paco?"

"I am fine Danilo! I wanted to take you all to the colony of the monkeys as we had agreed. Are you ready?" Paco responded with a smile.

"Do you feel okay swimming?" Danilo followed up with his question.

"Yes, I do! I came today to see you so I swam with no problem! Let's go, friend!" Paco responded.

Then, just as they heard Paco's words, Ernie commanded Andre and Danilo by saying, "Okay…Okay…Let's go! Let's take the life vests and sit down on the boat. We will follow you, Paco!"

"I'm ready to go," Danilo said quickly and rushed to the boat along with his dad and Andre. He walked quickly ahead of them, hoping they will get to the monkeys' colony sooner. He put on his sailing life jacket and his non-slippery shoes, and waved to Paco who already started moving, just as Ernie was starting the engine. Maybe, just maybe, this trip could save Carlo's life.

Chapter Five

Some moments never die. They determine how we believe and to what extent we follow through on what is significant. At that moment, everyone sat on the boat to pursue his belief, his mission which is to get Carlo back safe.

A boat trip on the Sea of Bohol is always very pleasant, it has a charm of its own.

However, when a trip's purpose is to search for a missing boy, it will be full of emotion, fear of the unknown, unexpected adventures, and unusual turns.

Before turning the engine, "I brought in with us a first aid kit, just in case. It contains motion sickness medication, antihistamine medicine for allergies, disinfectant, decongestant, and fever and pain medicine. Just let me know if you need help!" Ernie told Andre and Danilo.

"Very importantly, please wear your hat to protect yourself from the sun, as it can get very hot and you can be exposed to ultraviolet 'UV' rays than usual. You will need to protect your skin and head from those harmful rays (UV radiation is present in sunlight and constitutes about 10% of the total electromagnetic radiation output from the Sun). Let's all be careful; we do not want more problems," Ernie added.

The small wooded fishing boat smells of fish. Ernie and his brothers painted the boat in blue color some time ago. On its floor, you can find some small nets and an empty bucket that Ernie left it there. The boat was built to be used for fishing and not for taking trips; using it for a journey will be inconvenient. It also has no room for a walk-around besides it was rolling side to side, up, and down in a bobbing motion.

As the engine started and the boat sailed quickly behind Paco, Danilo's eyes stared at Paco while his mind was focused on Carlo. Then, the sun was shining brightly over the calm seawater.

On their way, there were many fishers fishing everywhere, sailing boats moving passengers to various parts of the Island, dolphins chasing ships, and seabirds chirping and chasing boats everywhere. The water of the Bohol Sea was clear and the scenery of the Tuna fishers catching the big fish was memorable.

A moment later, "Do you know that this sleek big Tuna that the three fishermen just caught is called 'Yellowfin'? They usually haul it using sustainable methods. They will then carefully store it in an icebox. Next to Indonesia, the Philippines is Asia's largest tuna exporter," Ernie was saying but wasn't sure if others were listening.

With no geographical destination in mind, Ernie had no choice but to follow Paco's lead.

Paco was moving north of the town; he was swimming away from the shores, apparently to avoid fishing nets, plastics, and other harmful objects left behind. Everyone on the boat was prepared for an unprecedented adventure while all the eyes were on Paco!

"It is hot, please drink more water," said Ernie as he handed water bottles to Danilo and Andre.

But beyond the bustle of the Sea of Bohol, the graceful panorama of the Island unfolded.

The dark-brown series of the geological wonder Chocolates Hills loomed in the distance like a mighty sentinel over the lush jungle and coastal plain.

As the boat sailed behind Paco, a gentle breeze was blowing all over, Danilo was trying to rest when images etched into his mind. Sometimes when he would prefer to forget it, they rose in vivid real-time. He can still remember meeting the old lady who gave him and Carlo corn, meeting Mother Monkey on the coconut farm, entering the Hills, meeting the tarsiers, watching Carlo's becoming a tarsier, living in the monkeys' colony, and coming home on Paco's back.

Danilo turned himself to the side of the boat and put both hands on the upper edge of the boat's side just as a wave hit the boat and sprayed everyone with foam. He tried his best to avoid looking at the looming Hills. One image dominated others; it persisted over time, however, did not provide a clear understanding of what he experienced when living for sometimes as a tarsier. He can only remember watching other tarsiers circulate them while chirping and feeling the changes on his body as he watched Carlo's body change as they both were terrified.

Danilo more than anyone else understands how precious life is. That moment was a time of reflection and realization, he was reflecting on his close ties to Carlo and realized more than any time ever the anticipation of joy and, paradoxically (an adverb here which means, in a seemingly absurd or self-contradictory way) the anguish of pain and the fear of losing a friend.

The image of Mother Monkey's response to his request in helping save Carlo does not leave his mind. He recalled her facial expressions when she squeezed her inward slanting eyebrows together, raised her chin, her big lips pressed together, frowning, and her large lips twisted to one side with a crease on the cheek. She was in total disagreement.

Danilo also remembered Mother Monkey's words, "I will be in big trouble with the Evil Giant of the Hills and his army of tarsiers if I got closer. They are out on the look for both of us. The Evil Giant and his tarsiers' army are very upset these days, they also have a very good sense of smell, and they can sense me quickly. It'll be a losing battle for me and for whoever goes there from my own family." The image of her frowning on her large lips, as she was responding to his request to save Carlo never left his mind.

"How she will receive us today? Will she be kind or…? She can be tough sometimes and have an attitude! I am not sure she will be friendly to my dad and Uncle Andre." Danilo was doing lots of self-talk.

"What it feel like if I am still in the Hills or the colony? What could have happened to me if Mother Monkey saved Carlo instead of me? Will they be looking for me now? Does Carlo remember us?" Danilo was mumbling to himself. With half-closed eyes, and eyebrows drew together, he was worried, thinking deeply, and enervated. He was trying hard to keep awake.

Meanwhile, Ernie and Andre were keeping each other's company. Sometimes discussing fish and fishing and sometimes go back and discuss possibilities of finding the monkeys' colony and the hope of ultimately finding Carlo. In the meantime, the boat kept moving fast forward behind Paco.

"To me and my family, Carlo reflected an openness of spirit that is contagious and infectious; it made me realize the totality of purpose that love engenders. Life without Carlo will be very difficult for all of us," Andre told Ernie as he was sobbing quietly.

"Keep the faith, *mahal na kaibigan*," (a term to mean 'dear friend' in the local language) These simple words affected Ernie; he was in tears too.

After a minute of silence, "Um, all shores look-alike, would it be possible for a dolphin to find the exact location? If not, what can we do?" a worried Andre asked.

"I believe so; dolphins are one of the most intelligent animals. They have large brains that help make them smarter and more intelligent than other species. You can tell from Paco's interaction with us, don't you feel he is interacting with us like a human?" Ernie asked.

"The more we see reality," Ernie continued, "the more apt we are to make better decisions. Let's be positive and keep the focus for now my friend!"

Andre reacted by saying, "You are right my dear friend!"

A few minutes later, it unexpectedly started raining with some thunder and lightning. The thunder boomed and cracked as fireworks and rain pattered all over. The rain whipped around them, the wind howled, and some small waves splashed over the boat. It made Danilo and Ernie a little nervous. No one on the boat had a raincoat.

Ernie held firmly onto the steering wheel to avoid any drifting. The boat twisted a little bit to the sides.

"No need to worry! Just hold on to your bench and do not move. Let's manage with what we have, it'll stop raining soon! You will later dry out in no time; do not mind being wet for now," Ernie said as he was downplaying the effects of the thunder, the rain, or the lightning while taking a glance at the light clouds. The boat continued moving in the exact direction Ernie wanted it to move.

Luckily, the rain was not heavy nor they did get stormy winds! It only rained for about fifteen or twenty minutes.

"Please help yourself to some snack or food, it seems our friend Paco is also eating while swimming," Ernie suggested and asked them to go ahead and open the cooler and get some food for everyone. He handed them an *Embutido* Meatloaf sandwich, (an *embutido* is meatloaf with tomato and basil grilled cheese sandwich) potato chips, and a bottle of water.

All of the sudden, "Look everybody, Paco is circling. It seems that we have arrived. Let's see! This location is very close to the town of Inabanga." Ernie figured it out.

"Is that the right shore, Danilo?" Ernie asked.

"Yes, it is, Dad, this is the area where I used to swim in! This is it! This area as you will see is a wild and wet one."

"Are you sure, Son? All shores look alike!" Ernie questioned again.

"Yes, I am an extremely positive dad. This is where I spent most of my time living with monkeys. They live close by, within a thirty-minute walk from the shore," an excited Danilo replied.

"I Love you, Paco! I Love you, Paco! You are the best, my friend! You are the best!" Danilo was joyfully screaming.

Paco was whistling in various frequencies and spinning into the air, he meant to say something like, "This is the place, I am very happy to find it!" he kept spinning and whistling.

Ernie quickly circled the boat around, headed closer to the shore, turned off the engine, and tied the boat to a big rock.

At that moment, Danilo stood up in the middle of the boat. He was sweating. His sweat was not heat-related, but a scared, nervous sweat that made him shrink in fear of what might be happening next. He was moving slowly and tried to ignore the stress that went into his belly.

His father came closer, lowered his voice, and put his hand on Danilo's shoulders. "I don't mean to pry," he said. "But you seem to have a lot on your mind."

He leaned closer, his voice almost a whisper. "Things will be alright, Son."

"I am scared, Dad!" Danilo responded.

"It is meant to be, Son, let's move on and make the best out of what we can," Ernie said then hugged Danilo who was groaning (a term here that means a low-pitched cry of grief).

Danilo ran a hand over his eyes. Experiencing what he went through is not an easy thing to forget.

They quickly landed and went closer to Paco who was calmed down and waited to get hugs from everyone. They all hugged and thanked Paco. Danilo gave him a big kiss and said, "I love you, dear Paco! You saved my life!"

Paco wished that he could get out of the water and accompany them in the search for Carlo but this is not possible. Instead, he said, "I hope you have a good and safe journey, Danilo."

"Now you can go back and I will lead them from here on," Danilo suggested as Paco made a failed attempt at a smile.

An excited Paco started whistling again and spinning into the air, he meant to say something like, "I love you too, Danilo, see you soon." Paco kept spinning and then took off as Danilo, Andre, and Ernie waved goodbye! It was apparent that his spinning is not the same as usual. He is still weak.

This area seemed deserted! It looks like a lonely place on the island. There is no trace of people living there.

Everyone was sweating. Their shirts stuck to their chests, their shorts to their sweaty thighs; it was hot and humid.

"Let's carry the fruit boxes. Let's put our shirts at the bottom of these boxes as they seemed wet and easy to break," Ernie said and carried one box as Andre carried the second.

The road that leads to the colony is wild and full of mangroves (a mangrove is a shrub or small tree that grows in coastal saline or brackish water. The term is also used for tropical coastal vegetation consisting of such species).

They can hear the constant sound of a breeze, gently swaying in its caress (a phrase here to mean an act or expression of kindness) and the birds twittering and flying from tree to tree. They can hear the gentle gurgling of a small creek. The sunlight was making a beautiful reflection on the wetland, brightening up dead tree trunks where shelf fungus grows.

"You will need to be very careful as we go through these mangroves and swamps to get to the colony. Some areas are slippery or difficult to walk through," Danilo said.

"It is going to be a rough walk, especially when carrying a heavy box," Andre said. "We have no other option, let's be careful." He nodded and continued walking.

"I can help both of you and carry the box when you are tired," Danilo suggested.

"Thank you! It is okay, we are fine, Son! Let's keep going. You can walk ahead of us," Ernie answered.

"These mangroves are critical spawning, nursery, feeding, and transient shelter areas to hundreds of fish species, crustaceans, and invertebrates. They support an abundant and productive marine life," Ernie explained.

"Like all other animals, fish, shrimp, crabs, and other marine life in the sea need a safe place to grow, away from many predators. With their tangled and intricate root systems, mangroves are excellent nurseries, providing safe hiding places for young animals. The muddy water around them is rich in nutrients from decaying leaves and organic matter produced by the mangroves themselves and from the sediment that is trapped around the roots. Mangroves' leaves are also a source of food for fish, shrimps, crabs, and other marine animals," Ernie continued his explanations as they were having a rough time passing through the wetlands.

On their way, they can feel the insects in their mouth and eyes, their feet crunching on dirt, and tripping over roots and branches.

"Let me know if you are thirsty, there is a stream of fresh water on our way," Danilo said. "That will be great, Son! Let's stop by it," his dad agreed.

In a few minutes, they could hear the sound of water trickling from a stream. It was time to rest, wash, and drink as the boxes were heavy and everyone was exhausted. Seemed like everyone was ready to drop, he was on his last leg with no longer had the energy to continue walking.

"Are we there yet?" asked Ernie.

"Um…Um…now we are very close to the colony, I guess we will be there in less than five minutes," Danilo responded.

"Are you okay guys? Can you move on or do you need to rest more?" Ernie asked.

Anxious to be there, "Let's do it!" Andre said and quickly carried the box on his shoulder and started walking quickly behind Danilo.

"Do we have to protect ourselves from the monkeys? Will they be friendly to us?" Andre asked Danilo.

"No need to worry, *tiyo* (a word that means 'Uncle' in their local language)," Danilo answered, "they are very friendly and good-hearted monkeys," Danilo added.

The trio continued their difficult journey in the wild and wetland. Carrying the fruit boxes that what made their journey more difficult. The cartoon boxes containing their fruit gift to monkeys were being torn because of being exposed to rain. Ernie and Andre tried hard to keep the contents intact with their shirts at the bottom. However, bananas and other fruits started falling and that was delaying their walk. Danilo continued picking up the falling fruit items from the ground and placed them in his shirts. He made a bag out of his shirts by tightening its sleeves.

In a few minutes, they could not help ignoring the grunting of the monkeys. "We are there now; we are on the outskirts of the colony," Danilo affirmed.

Chapter Six

After years of a father's loving relationship with Carlo, Andre could not be able to forget his son. He could not forget him wrestling playfully on the floor with his siblings', running outside the house after their dog, or tending to their chickens and roosters.

Andre was reflecting on his son's social and loving character with everyone. He recalled Carlo's image of smiling and collapsing into laughter when hearing something funny.

At that moment, Danilo was reflecting on his special friendship with Carlo, and the image of the smiling bass drummer who looks like Carlo who Danilo imagined him being Carlo appealing for his help to save him from the Hills suddenly came to mind. Other images persisted.

On the other hand, Ernie's mind was focused on what they might be able to do next. He also understood the ties that bind a father or mother to his or her son or daughter. He understood the bond of the child to his or her parents, siblings, or other family members. He had experienced this bond firsthand.

Now is a defining moment! The hope of being happy and bringing someone's life to the family lies in the ultimate, still to be realized of getting back Carlo safe.

In a few moments, the monkeys came rushing down, jumping all over Danilo, his dad, and Andre. They were on top of their shoulders, knocking the fruit boxes to the ground, and grabbing what they could grab from whatever box. In no time, all fruits were scattered on the ground and the monkeys were busy eating and fighting over them. However, the monkeys did not forget their friend, Danilo, they were jumping all over him, hugging him, and kissing him while eating what he brought in.

Then, Mother Monkey was cuddling with the baby monkeys, then quickly rushed to greet Danilo, Ernie, and Andre when she noticed their presence. She knew that he would be coming to visit one day but not that quickly. She stared at him with her gleaming eyes and brought him into a warm embrace. Danilo could have remembered how he felt when he said goodbye to her last time. He noticed again how her blood was pumping in her veins and the warm breath coming off her mouth as she moved her large cheek and big lips that look like the plunger.

"Mwah! Mwah! Mwah!" Mother Monkey gave Danilo three kisses on his head that sounded as if his dad was using the plunger on the kitchen sink.

Afterward, Mother Monkey stared at Danilo's dad, and at Andre, she shook their hands and gave them hugs.

"This is my dad; his name is Ernie! And this is Uncle Andre; he is the father of my best friend Carlo who you had met before," Danilo told Mother Monkey.

Nodding her head, Mother Monkey said, "It is my pleasure meeting you! I am happy you came to visit us. Thank you for your gift!"

Mother Monkey made a loud grunt as she starred at other monkeys who were still making a mess and fighting for the bananas and other fruits, "Bloom…Bloom…Tchawaaa…Waaa…Waaa!" which she probably meant something along the lines of "I am upset…I am upset, what you are doing is embarrassing!" Mother Monkey outstared them (a phrase which here means to look straight at someone's face for a long time until they can no longer look back at you).

Later, Mother Monkey sat on a tree stump and quietly asked with a smile, "How was your trip? Did you come swimming or walking?"

Ernie smiled back and said, "It was not bad, it was about the two-hour boat ride. We got on my little fishing boat. Perhaps someday I can take you out with your family on the sea for a little boat ride."

"Shinga lo! Phongo pengo?" Mother Monkey shrieked, which probably meant something like "How can you fit all of us on your little boat? You'll need a ship to fit us all." Ernie did not know what to say, he just maintained a shy smile.

Mother Monkey said, "O my son, Danilo! I had never expected to see you again!" While she uttered these words, she wept bitterly, and Danilo moved closer to her, mingled his tears with hers.

"I missed you, my son!" Mother Monkey told Danilo; that she was in the state of being under a spell (a phrase that here means a state of enchantment).

"Is there anything I can do to help?" Mother Monkey asked.

"We are here to kindly ask you to help us in getting Carlo back," Danilo responded; he was shivering.

"Please…Please! Please, help us!" Danilo begged her and continued shivering.

A desperate Carlo's dad who was emotional and in tears pled to Mother Monkey for help, "We have no one to help us find our son but you, dear Mother Monkey. I beg you to help us!" Andre cried. At that moment, Ernie was mute, yet he was in tears.

The silence following Danilo and Andre's impassioned requests was dramatic. Mother Monkey started shaking her face, her large lips twisted to the right side with an apparent crease on her cheek; hearing the request, made her panic. Her dark eyes were quite sunken into her skull, making her high cheekbones very prominent; Mother Monkey groaned inwardly (a phrase which here means she did not express her feeling; however, she made a deep sound in response to her agony) then bit her nails excessively and suddenly paced (a phrase that here means walked without purpose). Her eyes blinked and her big lips pursed; Mother Monkey was holding her mouth shut.

Watching her, everyone got scared. Danilo thought then screamed his question afterward, "Did he die?"

He got no answer from Mother Monkey.

Her unpredictable behavior gave way to fear. She paused instead and did not move a bit.

She did not mean bad, but her voice was sharp, and Danilo cried harder.

"Calm down, Son! Do not jump to any conclusion," his father yelled quietly at Danilo.

Danilo shook his head and started crying. His muffled sobs were apparent to all. His cries led his monkeys' brothers and sisters to come quickly to hug him. For a few moments, Danilo blinked up at the blue sky, furious and amazed, catching his breath.

But when she saw Danilo's gloomy face, she could see why he shrieked. She could feel his pulse start to race.

Mother Monkey was getting very emotional as she watched Danilo cry. He still remembers her exact words from the past, "I will be in big trouble with the Evil Giant of the Hills and his army of tarsiers if I got closer…they also have a very good sense of smell, they can sense me quickly."

Danilo came closer to Mother Monkey and sat on bended knees. "Please, Mother Monkey, please! Please get us, Carlo. Please!" Danilo shut his eyes tightly.

Suddenly, both of her eyes grew shiny, Mother Monkey slapped her hand in her palm and nodded in Danilo's direction, and said, "Oh, I'd love to do that," she uttered aloud.

"Although I know that my life and my family will be in dire danger, I will do that. I will search for Carlo! I am asking you to give me a few moments so I can think of how to do it!" Mother Monkey said and went into a state of mute. She had an earnest look in her eyes.

She kept quiet for over ten minutes giving thought to herself, "Bongashoon!" which meant something along the lines of 'well!'

"I will need to go and meet the Wise Monkey for advice, he is sensible, insightful, and knowledgeable; listening to him will be prudent."

"Just wait for me here, I will be back before sunset. Moreover, it will be a good opportunity for you to play with your monkeys' brothers and sisters," Mother Monkey said and quickly grabbed a hand of bananas, it is her gift to the Wise Monkey; then she slumped out of the colony, heading to meet the Wise Monkey.

The journey to the Wise Monkey's colony takes about two hours through a wild tropical jungle in which no paved roads or routes exist; instead, the jungle is full of lowland rainforest trees. It is a tough journey for Mother Monkey, she has to go through an area that is full of climbing vines, epiphytes (an organism that grows on the surface of a plant and derives its moisture and nutrients from the air, rain, and water, or debris accumulating around it), and open grassland. This jungle is a green habitat full of moss with a raw, earthy scent of wet mud in some areas and the sweet scent of forest flowers speckling the ground in bells of white and sprigs of lavender in other areas.

Additionally, this jungle contains various animals, including, wild hogs, deer, wild carabaos (a domestic swamp-type water buffalo), monkeys, civet cats, and various rodents (a gnawing mammal that includes rats, mice, squirrels, hamsters, porcupines (large rodents with coats of sharp spines, or quills, that protect them against predation), and others in the same families of mammal). In addition to mammals, the jungle is a home for many breeding species of birds such as megapodes 'turkey-like wildfowl', buttonquails, jungle fowls (wild birds such as duck, turkey, or pheasant), peacocks pheasant, doves, pigeons, parrots, and other birds. As it is full of wetlands, the jungle has many crocodiles and the larger snakes include pythons and various cobras.

Mother Monkey has to be very careful navigating the jungle; the journey might be dangerous; she needs to avoid wild mammals and snakes. She is particularly scared of crocodiles, larger snakes, wild hogs, wild carabao, and civet cats. Walking in the jungle is not as safe as someone might think! She does not usually go out late and knows that she needs to get back before dusk; the jungle could get more dangerous in dark. Mother Monkey sadly remembers her late husband known to all as Father Monkey was out in the forest one day and never made it back.

The path is soft beneath her feet, a mixture of soil, fallen leaves, wet grass, and moss.

Walking there could be very peaceful and relaxing if it was not for the wild animals. The ground was dark and damp. The curled brown leaves were half-embedded in it, trampled by the occasional dog walker, and the small prints of animals, rodents, and birds. Mother Monkey can breathe, fill her lungs, and exhale the jungle's fresh air.

Like other monkeys, Mother Monkey is not as fast as bullet trains or cars; however, she is capable of moving remarkably at a high speed of about 30 miles/hour. She was running fast using all four limbs and her flat palms in her climbing, walking, or running.

After almost two hours or so of relentless walking, running, and climbing through the wild jungle, she arrived at the outskirts of the Wise Monkey's colony, the journey had sapped her and left her exhausted. After drinking and resting for a few minutes by a water stream, she went inside the big colony that contained over fifty monkeys who live and serve the Wise Monkey, some were members of his own family.

As she entered the colony, the Wise Monkey appeared leaning back in his wooded seat eating while surrounded by other monkeys. Before she prostrated herself before him (a phrase, which here means submission or adoration), she wanted to present the bananas as a token of appreciation and respect. She approached him and said, "I brought to your honor this hand of bananas, would Your Honorable Wise Monkey accept it?"

"Um, it is my pleasure to accept your gift, please hand it to my assistant, take your seat, and wait for your turn," the Wise Monkey answered and ordered his assistant to take the bananas and bring them to him. His assistant did exactly what the Master ordered and then returned to his seat on a tree stump next to his Master 'The Wise Monkey'.

Afterward, Mother Monkey placed herself before the Wise Monkey and sat quietly on the ground awaiting His Honorable Wise Monkey to listen to what she had to say or ask.

Back in Mother Monkey's colony, Danilo, Ernie, and Andre were impatiently looking for Mother Monkey's return. While waiting, Danilo was playing and running around with his monkeys' brothers and sisters as some monkeys were bathing with each other as part of their socialization, a couple was resting on trees, and some were still eating fruits, leaves, twigs, and other plants.

At the same time, the Wise Monkey was so much taken up by the many requests from those who were attending on all of his sides. Some of them asked questions, while others were telling him things. The honorable Wise Monkey as the monkeys call him was advising in instances or telling the asking monkey, "You'll need to come back and see me tomorrow; I need to think about what you asked!"

Mother Monkey started feeling that the Wise Monkey was getting heartily tired, for he stood suddenly and ordered those who were waiting to speak to him to leave his colony and come back the next day. At then, Mother Monkey started to lose her patience; she was extremely fatigued from waiting so long. Nevertheless, she had no choice; she will go back early the next day; perhaps the Wise Monkey may not be as busy.

Going back to her colony is as dangerous as going to the Wise Monkey's colony. As she was tired, she knows that she needed to get home before dusk. Being late could jeopardize her safety. No errors or slight direction mistake is appropriate at this time of the day. Going in the wrong direction will delay her trip and could prove costly. Mother Monkey was getting her gasping breath in the silence. She was stepping over any fallen tree, regardless of its type or bark! She was jumping fast over trees with smooth bark, rough bark, peeling bark, or rotting bark. Her objective was to get back before dark.

As it was getting late, Danilo, Ernie, and Andre started getting worried that she was in danger or got hurt. Mother Monkey was gone for too long and the jungle has many wild animals.

They were watching the monkeys playing and socializing via vocalization. They were using a variety of sounds to socialize. Sometimes low chatter, clicking, and sometimes high pitch yelling can be heard for long distances. Some monkeys were using non-verbal communication to show emotion. A mom was snuggling her baby. On the other side, they stared at some adult monkeys sitting close to each other and touching each other's faces as a means of socialization.

Later on, a noise came from behind the bushes; seemed like Mother Monkey just arrived!

She was sweating and her throat went tight. She told herself to relax, drink a little, and take a breath. Everyone was anxious to hear what she had to say.

After taking a deep breath, she told them what happened and suggested the trio 'Danilo, Ernie, and Andre' could stay in the colony or go home and come back on the second day.

"Thank you, honorable Mother Monkey, for what you did, we appreciate you very much," said Ernie and suggested they go back as their family will be waiting and will be worried if they don't go back today.

"Can Danilo stay with us?" asked Mother Monkey.

"Thank you, dear Mother Monkey, if Danilo stays here, he will be missed by his mom. That makes it difficult, especially after what he went through! I hope, he will do so in the future as we are all becoming closer to you and your family," Ernie responded.

"I understand…Good night," said Mother Monkey, she finally agreed, and then waved goodbye. Other monkeys jumped and waved too.

It was time to go back to Calape before it gets dark; they needed to go through the mangroves on their way to the shore. Going through it in the dark will be difficult and dangerous, no one carries a flashlight, and Ernie's flashlight was kept on his boat. Branches were also getting in their faces and tearing their clothes in instances as they walk.

As it was getting dark, they could still hear the gentle gurgling of the small creek mixed with the sounds of the various creatures pursuing each other. At the same time, frogs were croaking, wolves were howling from a distance and owls started hooting. This wild wetland hides all the animals that drink from that creek.

"Let's hurry up and move as fast as we can," Ernie said.

Quickly, all of them started walking and then running fast to reach the shore as early as they could. It was much easier to go back as they did not have any carry-on.

After almost half an hour of walking through the wetland, they reached the shore and got on the boat. It was dusk, the sun had just set. Ernie turned on the boat's engine and said, "It will take us about an hour and a half to get to Calape, I will use my emergency flashlight when needed."

Operating a boat in the dark is not easy, as it is difficult to see much of anything, including what you're about to hit if you get unlucky. The good thing, Ernie is an experienced fisherman and boat navigator, he had been boating long enough and knows how to navigate in the dark. Regardless, he needs to be careful!

Danilo was staring at the blackness of the night sky while Andre was keeping Ernie company by constantly talking to him. As for Ernie, his goal was to bring everyone back safely! His concerns were going way beyond watching ahead, he cannot even take a glance away from watching the boat route, the task at night is more difficult than during daylight, and pair of eyes must always be directed to the route and nothing else. He was using the flashlight in some instances and slowing down in other instances. Using more light at night on the boat kills your night vision.

"We shouldn't use much light, the light on the boat reduces our ability to see beyond; our eyes automatically adjust to the amount of light available to them. To be prudent, I'll have to slow down a little bit, it will take some 30 minutes or so longer. Let's be safe than sorry!" said Ernie.

"Not a problem, *mahal na kaibigan* (a term to mean 'dear friend' in the local language)."

Going back on the boat was serene at this time, there were not many boats in the sea and everyone was calm but felt hopeful!

After almost two hours in the sea, they arrived in Calape. Ernie quickly docked his boat and, in a few minutes, they were on their way home where everyone in their families was waiting to hear the news.

Upon arriving home, Andre needed to calm his wife, his parents, and his kids. He urged them to keep their hope alive! He told them all the details of his day-long journey and that he will be going on the next day. Meanwhile, Cora was awaiting her husband and son, they told her what had happened and urged her to keep the faith!

Chapter Seven

The next morning after sunrise, Mother Monkey started her journey back to the Wise Monkey's Colony. Upon her arrival, she appeared exhausted, as the journey was too long.

She ran toward the front line where everyone sat facing the Wise Monkey as if she is more important than others or as if she were on a special mission.

After waiting for a little while, the Wise Monkey walked in straight to his seat on the tree stump, surrounded by a staff of six monkeys who acted as his servants and security guards. The staff usually keep his company all day long and make sure that his day runs as smoothly as possible.

Although Mother Monkey has great courage and charisma, she was a bit nervous because everyone had told her the Wise Monkey was a powerhouse. Therefore, when she was ready to lay her pitch on him, he was not ready to hear as a few monkeys surrounding him were talking loudly. As soon as she said, "Hello, your honorable Wise Monkey." He jumped out with, "Hey, Mother Monkey! I am happy to see you again. Thank you for the gift you brought me yesterday, it was delicious. How are you today?" the Wise Monkey compassionated her for having waited for so long, asked her to come closer, and said, "What business brings you here? Please tell me your story. Please say what's on your mind?"

"I beg, your honorable Wise Monkey, to assure me first of your willingness to help save someone's life."

"Okay." He shrugged, then looked at her with passion. "Well," replied the Wise Monkey, "I will guide you and help you in whatever means that I have, and no harm shall come to you. I will need first to know the full story and what brought you to see me. Tell me what you'll need to tell me." Wise Monkey's staff and others were quietly listening.

When Mother Monkey sensed his compassion and sincerity, she told the Wise Monkey what she knows regarding what happened to Danilo and Carlo and what she did so far.

The Wise Monkey did not give Mother Monkey enough time to finish her story, and said, "Thank you for sharing much-needed details, and I have gotten a very good idea and have heard enough!" Then the Wise Monkey stopped talking and remained for some time motionless with admiration.

"I beg your honorable Wise Monkey once more to help save Carlo, not only for me but for his suffering family and friends."

"Tell me about Father Monkey, your husband! The Wise Monkey asked her."

Mother Monkey took a deep breath, her eyes were watering, she sobbed, and her voice was cracking with emotion.

"Ah…Um…Ah…Um…Ah…What can I tell Your Honorable Wise Monkey about him? He left the colony some time ago as soon as the sun rose to look for another source of food for us during the dry season."

Mother Monkey kept crying and added while trying to calm down, "We waited for him until the sunset, then I had no other choice but to go out and look for him everywhere…I wasn't able to find him. Instead, I found the two boys at the corn farm. As for my husband, he never made it back!"

Then, the Wise Monkey closed his eyes for a moment, took a deep breath, a short silence, and spoke in muted tones saying, "You are an honorable mother and honorable being, and I am willing to help! I am amazed by your passion and commitment to helping others." He was very compassionate.

After having prostrated himself on the ground, the Wise Monkey said, "Dear, Mother Monkey, I have some good advice to give you."

"I'm here to listen to what you will tell me, your Honorable Wise Monkey! I will record every piece of advice in my mind," she replied.

The Wise Monkey asked all to be silent, and then he closed his eyes for a moment, took a deep breath one more time, and said, "The reality of our life and destiny plays an important role in what we do. You can't be sure of your success or failure; you can only prepare for what you have to do with all of your heart and consciousness. If you do so, you will have the edge. If not, you will bring about defeat unless you are very lucky, and there is little chance for luck here. It will not be smart to fight a battle that you cannot win!

Accordingly, my first advice is for you to properly plan! You are about to have a major confrontation with the Evil Giant of the Hills."

After a brief silence, the Wise Monkey added, "My second advice is to choose your fighters who will be fighting the Evil Giant very carefully and with great care and consideration. They need to be tough and loyal to ensure victory. One important thing here that you should remember is that you should also know what it is you wish to accomplish and how."

"After you choose your fighters," the Wise Monkey added, "you will need to explain to them the purpose, get their commitment, and show them how to accomplish the mission. This is my third piece of advice."

"My fourth advice, dear Mother Monkey, is to treat all of your fighters as equals and make sure each one of them feels special. Accordingly, I ask you to be compassionate with them, ensure their safety, and make sure you have enough food for them. Your fighters need to eat and be safe. Do not make them suffer, it brings their morale down," the Wise Monkey continued.

"Going into the battlefield-meaning going to the Chocolate Hills to bring the missing boy must ensure that all preparations are in place and there's no room for a mistake. If there is a possibility of a mistake, revisit your plan. This is my fifth piece of advice to you, honorable Mother!" The Wise Monkey kept talking.

"In addition, I want to leave you with a bit of a piece of advice that I inherited from my father who learned from our ancestors. This could be my best advice and your path to victory. So, listen carefully," the Wise Monkey said, his eyes opened wide, and smiled. "Your efforts can be minimized by using a key tool of battle – deception. You must look busy doing something else when in fact you and your fighters are working intelligently against the enemy, the Evil Giant. You will need to keep your enemy off balance! Remember not to underestimate your enemy or feel that he is incapable of destroying you and your fighters. Think intelligently and create disturbances or situations that keep him on the move and make him lose focus instead. This is my best sixth piece of advice for you." Afterward, he stopped talking and then closed his eyes!

Suddenly, he asked everyone present to keep silent, as he needed to meditate for a few minutes with no disturbance. All listened and sat quietly as they watched him staring at the blue sky in silence. Afterward, he closed his eyes for a few more minutes and then said, "Today, I want to give you a big secret! A secret is a secret, it must be kept secret! An eclipse of the sun will be happening after six sunrises 'after six days'. When an eclipse happens, the Evil Giant's power will be weakened. His leadership ability and command of the tarsiers will be diminished as long as the eclipse lasts. My best advice, take advantage of the eclipse and plan accordingly. A good leader knows when to attack, you seem to be a good leader, Mother Monkey!"

"An eclipse…? What do you mean by that, your honor? I have never heard of it," said Mother Monkey.

"During a solar eclipse, the Moon casts two shadows toward Earth. One shadow is called the umbra, which becomes smaller as it reaches the Earth. This is the dark center of the Moon's shadow. The second shadow is called the penumbra. This shadow becomes larger as it reaches the Earth. Only those who live in the area covered by the umbra can see a total solar eclipse or a complete blocking out of the Sun's light. People who live in the area of the Earth covered by the penumbra will see a partial eclipse," the Wise Monkey answered her as everyone nodded her or his head in agreement and as a way to express respect.

"We are living in the area that is covered by the umbra, (during an eclipse, two shadows are cast. The first is called the umbra, this shadow goes away from the sun and gets smaller. It is the dark center of the eclipse shadow)," the Wise Monkey added.

"My last advice to you before leaving, I want to remind you not to show signs of fear regardless of what the circumstances are, it will bring your fighters' morale down while uplifting the enemy's morale. Keep their morale high!" the Wise Monkey said and asked her to tell him if she has any more questions or concerns.

"Thank you for your excellent advice, your honorable Wise Monkey! Well, I guess I haven't been using my head and giving my options enough thought," she confided to him.

"You have begun," the Wise Monkey noted, "by taking the first step of thinking through to save the boy. The first important question that you should be asking yourself is, am I able to save Carlo, and think it through?"

Mother Monkey wanted to know more and asked, "How do I discover which is my best plan?"

"Well, I guess I could ask myself…Will this plan best help me to save Carlo?"

"That's an excellent question," the Wise Monkey said. "You are on the right track now, good luck!"

Then the Wise Monkey smiled and added, "I'll bet you will be able to execute your plan well."

As Mother Monkey looked into the face of the honorable Wise Monkey who was presenting his ideas and answering her concerns, she felt more relaxed that she will be able to think through an excellent plan and do a good job.

"Thank you, Honorable Wise Monkey. I will leave you in peace now if you allow me to excuse myself and go back to my colony and start planning," Mother Monkey said and stood up.

"One more thing you should know before you leave today," said the Wise Monkey, "you need to avoid harming tarsiers or eating them. Paradoxically (a term that means, the more we know, the more we identify an increasing number of questions to which we have no answers as yet), our ancient superstition that we inherited from our ancestors coupled with relatively thick rainforest and ills, has preserved tarsiers. We have been instructed by our ancestors to leave tarsiers in the wild because we fear that these animals could bring bad luck. One belief passed down from ancient times is that they are pets belonging to spirits dwelling in the dark hollow close to the ground or near the trunk of trees."

"If we harm them," added the Wise Monkey, "we will need to apologize to the spirits of the forest and the Hills, or we will encounter sickness or hardship in life. As I wish you the best of luck, go back to your family and start planning." He waved his hands and stood up in respect to Mother Monkey. Mother Monkey bowed in respect and left in a hurry.

On her way back, the rainfall created dark and damp wet ground. While passing the ancient rough trees that had been worn down by the soft greenness of moss, Mother Monkey was only thinking of what the Wise Monkey has told her.

"I need to make a plan…a good plan. I need to move fast, I have only six more sunrises (6 days) before the eclipse happens," Mother Monkey was doing her usual self-talk.

She remembered and reflected on Wise Monkey's opening statement, "The reality of our life and destiny plays an important role in what we do. You can't be sure of your success or failure; you can only prepare for what you have to do with all of your heart and consciousness. If you do so, you will have the edge. If not, you will bring about defeat unless you are very lucky, and there is little chance for luck here. It will not be smart to fight a battle that you cannot win! Accordingly, my first advice is for you to properly plan!"

Upon her arrival at the colony, Danilo, Ernie, and Andre were waiting there along with Mother Monkey's family.

"Happy to see you again, Mother Monkey," said Danilo.

"Me too, I am happy to see you all!" Mother Monkey responded she was exhausted. Her heart was beating fast and there was a pulsing in her head and limbs. She gasped and blinked at the sky as she tried to catch her breath then stared at everyone and shouted, "Leave me alone, do what you want to do but be quiet, I need to think!" Mother Monkey ordered everyone before she headed toward a large tree to lie under so she can comfortably think about her plan.

Upon laying down, she took a deep breath and then stared at the blue sky for a moment to relax her mind and think clearly. She acted conceited.

"The Wise Monkey wanted me to properly plan. He advised me to choose my fighters very carefully with great care and consideration…Um, he advised me to explain the purpose, get my fighters' commitment, and show them how to accomplish the mission. I also remember he told me to treat them equally and make sure all feel they are special. What else? Ah…He wanted me to be compassionate and make sure I got them enough food and…Ah, I remember! He wanted me to ensure that there's no room for a mistake, to keep the enemy off balance, to use deception, and avoid harming tarsiers. Have I forgotten anything?"

"Um…Um…He also advised me to not engage in a battle that I cannot win," Mother Monkey was doing some sort of self-talk.

"We monkeys are known for our intelligence and wisdom, I will teach the Giant Evil a lesson that he will never forget," Mother Monkey kept talking to herself.

As she was thinking and reflecting, an idea had come to her. She had tried to think creatively and told herself to be careful in taking a risk. Yet she could not let the idea of saving Carlo goes away.

Chapter Eight

In the late afternoon, Mother Monkey came back and sat down on her designated tree stump, called everyone to come close, then said, "I have had a productive day with His Honorable Wise Monkey and we have agreed on a few great bits of advice that I need to execute to save Carlo. For us, time is of the essence as I need to move fast. I need everyone's cooperation, are you in agreement?"

"Yes, we are!" the monkeys and others – Danilo, Ernie, and Andre shouted in agreement. "Danilo and parents," said Mother Monkey, "I need you to go right back to your town and get me some of Carlo's used clothes and other personal items by tomorrow, the dirtier the clothes and items are, the better it would be! Don't ask me why! Just do what I've asked you to do and come back."

"One more thing," Mother Monkey added, "I will need you to bring food for all of us on the sixth sunrise 'sixth day' as our plan to go to the Hills on the day after the sixth sunrise 'meaning the seventh day', so I'll need enough food to feed my family on that day."

"Okay, we will leave now," Danilo responded, shook her hand to say goodbye, waved to other monkeys, and walked out. Ernie and Andre nodded, shook her hand, waved to other monkeys, and walked away with Danilo. They were on their way to go back to the boat and then to their hometown.

Later on, Mother Monkey called five of her strongest monkeys and said, "You are my strongest and fiercest fighters! I am going to organize you into four patrols consisting of six monkeys each. Each one of you will be leading and protecting five of your brothers and sisters while following my orders. You will be my generals and my senior council, we will meet at every sunrise to discuss the plan," Mother Monkey added as she brought both of her hands together, showing complete togetherness.

"Are you willing to do whatever you can to support my plan while protecting your patrol members?" Mother Monkey asked as all nodded their heads in agreement.

"How about our babies?" asked someone.

"The three babies that we currently have in our colony will be kept here with one of the mothers to care for them. All others will join us," she answered.

In a few minutes, they collectively decided how to divide evenly the colony members into four patrols of six members each. Each leader knows who is in her or his troop.

"We will soon be on a mission to save the other boy from the Hills, which requires us to work as a team. Knowing that we're all going to face danger trying to save the boy, our mission will be easier if we coordinate better and you protect your troop. Their safety is a priority, you will need to guard them against any threat and ensure their safe exit from the Hills when I order you to do that. If I am hurt, one of you will take the lead!"

She pointed her hands toward one of the five monkeys and said, "You are the one who I designate to be my assistant and the next in line leader to take over the mission! Are you willing?" Mother Monkey asked him.

"Yes, I am willing to take over the mission, dear Mother, however, I hope nothing happens to you," he answered her.

"I will call you the Second in Command Leader, going forward," she said and everyone cheered him.

"As a part of the plan, we will need to go out on the sixth sunrise 'sixth day', that is the day before our mission to find *Sampaguita* flower. *Sampaguita* is a flower that resembles the Confederate jasmine vine commonly found in the United States, the *Sampaguita 'Jasminium sambac'* is the national flower of the Philippines. Small star-like flowers blossom in clusters amid waxy, green leaves. *Sampaguita* has a sweet, thick scent and is widely used for Asian tea blends. The *Sampaguita* symbolizes divine hope and is often used as a garland for social celebrations. We will need to pick it up and bring it to the colony," said Mother Monkey.

"We will need a lot of this flower. You will take your troop members and let them help you pick it; I will be going with you to pick it too. Regardless, I will remind you of when to go," Mother Monkey told her patrols' leaders.

"Why do we need this flower, Mother?" one asked.

"Let me explain, my dear brave heroes. We will be using this flower as a tool to confuse the enemy by disguising our smell," said Mother Monkey and explained in detail how they'll use it to deceive the Evil Giant of the Hill. "We will explain to our monkeys the purpose later when we are ready to implement our plan," she added.

"Ha…Ha…Ha…" everyone laughs a loud after she explained the purpose of getting the flower in more detail.

"You are funny and very creative, this is a wonderful idea, Mother," one of the monkeys said while others cracked laughing.

"Very importantly, we will need to master our attack and assure its success. Let's divide the Hills into four parts, the Northeast, the Southeast, the Northwest, and the Southwest. Doing so will disrupt whatever defensive plan the enemy might have and force the uneven distribution of his power and attention. My Second Command Leader and I will advance toward the middle of the forest. Each of you will enter from one side and start doing crazy rituals in his or her assigned geographical area while sniffing the trees for the boy until we find him. This is our tool to succeed, it is another deception tool my dears," she added.

Mother Monkey closed her eyes for a moment, then said, "You'll enter your territory when I whistle, we all need to enter at the same time. If you reach your territory early, you wait for my order. As soon as someone identified the tree where the boy is, he or she must alert his or her troop's leader. Your job is to quickly validate and jump on the tree to get the boy. You should immediately whistle to us, have full control of the tarsier's boy as he will resist his capture, and you quickly run out with him while ensuring all of your members follow you," Mother Monkey explained then started drawing the plan and its map on the muddy ground using a tree stick so everyone can understand.

"We will make advances into the Hills as we feel certain there will be no resistance from the Evil Giant, from other wild animals, or any of his allies," Mother Monkey stated.

"If I feel that the time is not right, we will not go there. Additionally, if we go there and I sense that the Evil Giant is in a good shape, I will order you out," she continued assuring her patrols' leaders and her second-in-command leader.

She then took a deep breath and said, "The Wise Monkey gave me a secret that I will only share with you! He told me that an eclipse will happen after six sunrises (after six days). When it happened, the Evil Giant of the Hills will be weak at then."

"An eclipse? What does it mean?" asked one of the monkeys' leaders.

"Um...Um...I am not sure! However, I guess it means the sun will get her vacation and go to visit her family! I think this is what I had understood," Mother Monkey answered.

"How about if the sun did not go on vacation to visit her family?" asked another monkey leader.

"Therefore, we will not attack unless we see the eclipse. If there's a change in the shapes of the sun or the moon, we will change our plan too. We will not attack and we will need to re-think our strategy. I shall communicate with you on an ongoing basis," she answered.

"One more thing, all food will be brought before our mission. There will be no need for you to look for food. You will need to ensure that every member of your troop eats in the early morning. Ensure that he or she is not hungry after we leave here," said Mother Monkey.

"How about if they get hungry later?" asked another monkey leader.

"You'll need to make sure they take their food with them and eat when they get hungry in the Hills. We can't afford to have someone hungry, that will put her or him in low-spirit or intent, the enemy will take advantage of us," answered Mother Monkey.

Using this advice, I can predict victory. If we collaborate as a team and execute according to the plan, I foresee victory.

All five monkeys' leaders exhibited understanding and showed support and loyalty.

"Concerning the tarsiers, you must train and educate your troops' members to treat them with respect, they will not fear us, try to run away, or hurt us. Hurting others is always easier, but is also the costliest in terms of what we can do. Unless it is necessary, we shall never use force against any tarsier or animal while in the Hills. We are on a specific mission to bring the missing boy who looks like a tarsier, nothing else is important. We want to be on the tarsiers' best side!" said Mother Monkey.

"How to identify the tarsier's boy?" asked one monkey leader.

"Soon, we will get the boy's old clothes. We will all need to practice sniffing his scent through his used clothes or used items. That will be an easy way to locate him on the tree. We need to do a good job when sniffing as his scent is getting weaker by now," answered Mother Monkey.

"The key to our success is to keep practicing, we will need to overwhelm the Evil Giant and make him vulnerable. We will start practicing rituals for the sun every day and making a strange noise while looking toward the ecliptic sun. We will practice a strange dance that confuses the enemy and let him and others focus on these crazy rituals and not suspect us of doing something else," said Mother Monkey.

"One more thing before I go to sleep and rest a little bit, if any of us gets hurt, we will fight with conviction to save as much as we can our family members. You must lead and be a good example for your patrol members. I trust you all and have faith in every one of you. I believe you will be great leaders and we will collectively succeed in our mission. Our ancestors always beat the enemy when they plan well and foresaw victory. I can see victory with you! You can go now and do what you like to do," Mother Monkey said.

Quickly, she stood up, tilted her head back, took a deep breath, and yelled, "Stop…Stop! There's one more important thing you should know!" Mother Monkey then took another deep breath and said, "I want to stress the need for teamwork. We must function as one unit, one team! Teamwork and team spirit are prerequisites for our success and this starts with us, leaders! We will all need to be closer to our goal of bringing the kid back safely to his family. I want to ensure that all of our monkey family members accept our goal, work toward it, and follow orders! Doing so, ensure success and safety for all. You will need to make sure that no monkey exerts less individual effort on this important task! Let's preserve the culture of placing a high value on shared responsibility."

Mother Monkey closed her eyes and went into a deep siesta (a phrase that means here an afternoon rest or a nap, especially one taken during the hottest hours of the day in a hot climate).

Chapter Nine

It takes pressure to make a perfect idea or an ideal plan! Creativity and some great ideas need windows of time without pressure. However, there are always benefits from situations where the pressure gets in the way and makes things intense. Mother Monkey was pressured to act within a short time frame as the eclipse will be happening soon. Pressure time ignited her brain and put all of her focus on the mission to successfully carry out a plan to save Carlo.

It was a little before sunrise when Andre was getting ready to go to Ernie's home and accompany him and Danilo to the Monkeys' colony. That was the time they had agreed to meet and go back to see Mother Monkey. Carlo's family already packed Carlo's old clothes the night before so Andre, Ernie, and Danilo could take them along to the colony.

Before leaving the house, Carlo's mom gave her husband a big hug and wished him the best of luck. She wanted badly to see her lost son. Sonia was not able to control her tears.

Everyone is still hoping to find Carlo. Carlo's grandfather got very ill but was still hopeful to see his grandson one day.

After a ten-minute walk, Andre knocked on Danilo's family door and said, "*Magandang umaga kaibigan (Good morning, friend)*!"

"*Magandang umaga (Good morning), welcome Andre*!" Ernie responded upon opening the door. "We are ready, let's go…Let's hurry up, Danilo," Ernie added and, in a few minutes, they were on their way to the boat while carrying a big bag of Carlo's clothes.

Paco was waiting near the boat to say hi. As soon as they arrived, he started spinning and whistling. Danilo rushed to hug him while Ernie and Andre waved and blow kisses in the air.

The dolphin was happy but still in pain; he still looks ill.

In a few minutes, Ernie started the boat and headed to the monkeys' shore.

After two hours of sailing and then walking through the mangroves, they arrived at the colony. All monkeys came out running thinking they brought food, they started jumping up and down, tearing out the clothes box, and snatching the clothes. Very quickly, an upset Mother Monkey shouted and ordered all monkeys to stop, she rushed after them with a long stick. All monkeys climbed the trees to escape her stick; then they calmed down afterward.

"Good morning, dear Mother Monkey!" said Danilo and gave her a big hug. Ernie and Andre followed and did the same.

"Happy to see you and glad you brought your son's clothes," said Mother Monkey. "Thank you again for your help, Mother Monkey!" Andre responded, his face grinning out of control; he was expressing his appreciation and respect through a big smile.

"As I told you, you'll need to bring us food soon. As per my plan, I will need it after five sunrises – five days from now," said Mother Monkey.

"Food will be here, Mother Monkey, after five sunrises, do not worry!" Ernie said.

Then, strong vocalizing sounded like "Chooooona!" this probably meant, "Come on, it's time for training." This voice came from one older monkey who is Mother Monkey's Second Command Leader.

Quickly, all monkeys came running and surrounded the older monkey. Afterward, he started with the help of four other monkeys talking and dividing them into four groups. In a few minutes, all monkeys lined up in four rows behind their patrols' leaders as they were instructed. There was some noise coupled with other vocalizing sounds from patrol leaders before everyone sat down listening to the older monkey, who drew the four directions of the hills on the ground that showed the Northside, the Southside, the Eastside, and the Westside.

After a little while, he then added the other four directions to show the Northeast, Southeast, Northwest, and Southwest. He continued instructions and more explanations while Danilo, Ernie, and Andre were in total surprise and confusion.

Later on, "Chweeeya!" probably meant, "Go away, it's time for you to leave," the sound came out from the same adult monkey leader.

Mother Monkey showed her big smile; she was very happy seeing what she saw. Then, they all heard again "Chooooona!" she meant, "Come on, it's time for training." Then, monkeys came running in groups of five from four different directions, they lined behind their patrol leaders, and started performing dancing and rituals with unusual vocalization sounds as they were ordered to do.

Monkey patrol leaders burst with exuberance (a phrase that means they were in a state of high spirit, energy, and enthusiasm). Through their communication and leadership, those leaders brought other monkeys a lightning-fast pace and incredible motivation.

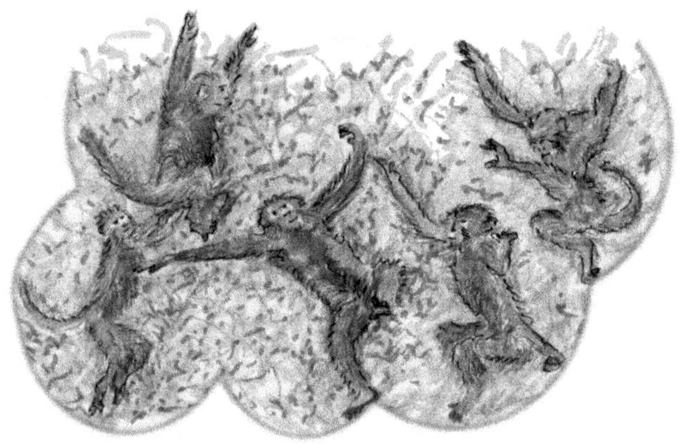

"What is this, Mother?" Danilo asked.

"This is something very important that we will use to save your friend," she answered.

A confused Danilo continued watching the unusual performance. He realized she does not want to explain further.

Later, the four patrol leaders brought Carlo's clothes and passed them to monkeys who started sniffing them one after another.

"Are you confused?" Mother Monkey asked.

"Yes, indeed! Wow! Wow! This is amazing but also confusing," answered Danilo as all were watching the four patrol leaders shrieking while other monkeys listen and obey their orders.

"I am happy to hear what you just saw is both amazing and confusing, my dear human son," said Mother Monkey, "That helps!" she added.

Suddenly, there came dark clouds hovered around the sky, giving everyone a warning that the rain will soon be starting.

"*Ang kahulugan ng iwanan natin ngayon*!" Ernie shrieked, (which meant 'let's leave now!')

"Goodbye, Mother Monkey, and see you after five sunrises. We will bring the food early in the day," said Ernie and they all walked away as all the other monkeys were busy performing their ritual drill.

Then it was the sixth sunrise, 'the sixth day' after Mother Monkey met the Wise Monkey. Tomorrow is the expected eclipse and the start of operations 'Rescue Carlo'.

The Calape's trio just arrived at the Mother Monkey's shore 'as they called it'. With them, they brought two boxes of bananas, two boxes of mangos, and the two boxes of fish that Ernie caught the day before.

I am not sure if you know that fruit is the primary food that monkeys consume. Those who live close to the coastal lines consume some fish too. Although the fruits are seasonal, monkeys move around their home habitat to find them. The mothers need to have enough food so that their bodies can produce milk for the young.

An interesting fact about monkeys' life, they often spread seeds from the fruits as they move along. This behavior is so important to the habitat. The spreading of the seeds helps to ensure future vegetation and monkeys' future food. Plants and leaves are all over their habitats too, they will eat them if they can't find fruit.

"How we are going to take it to the colony?" asked Andre.

"I suggest we keep it on the boat and we ask Mother Monkey for help. Probably, she will send out her monkeys to bring them up to the colony. They can manage!" suggested Danilo.

"I brought with me many plastic bags to make it easy to split the loads and for the monkeys to carry it," said Ernie. Additionally, "I suggest that Mother Monkey supervises the handling of the food as we do not want the monkeys to damage the boxes upon our arrival and start taking what we brought out of control," Ernie added. "So, let's only fill and carry only two plastic bags each containing a sample of what we have brought," Ernie added, then all walked toward the colony.

After half an hour of walking through the mangroves, they arrived at the colony. The dust was all over as the monkeys were running in groups and performing their new ritual training with their leaders.

As soon as she spotted them, Mother Monkey came out running to Ernie, Andre, and Danilo. Angry, she stomped her foot. The trio moved back quickly. However, she yanked her tail, slapped them on the face, and pushed them down to the ground; she appeared very upset and snobbish. They were surprised and scared, they had no clue why she did what she did. They were speechless!

In no time, she snapped one of the bags, threw its contents on the ground, and started kicking the mangos. An astonished Danilo got scared, cried, and trembled; his dad and Andre were disappointed and worried.

Suddenly, "*Bloom...bloom..., tooka doom*," which probably meant something along the lines of "I am upset...I am upset, go away!" Mother Monkey uttered, squeaked in a high-pitched voice, and screamed again saying, "I had asked you to bring enough food for all, this is not enough!"

"I beg your pardon, Mother Monkey, there seems to be a misunderstanding. Let me explain," Ernie said.

"No! No! *Bloom...bloom...cheka boom*! There's no misunderstanding!"

She replied, "I was clear on what I have asked you to bring," angrily reacted.

"Just give me a minute to explain," Ernie begged her to listen.

"What do you want to say?" She outstared them (a term that means here to look straight at someone's face for a long time until they can no longer look back at her) she said while she was still very upset.

"Mother Monkey, we brought more food with us. We kept it on the boat as we need yours and your family members to help us bring it up here," Ernie said.

"I am so sorry! Am sorry!" she calmed down and then covered her face with her hands; she was feeling bad about how she reacted.

Mother monkey stared at them with her gleaming eyes. She felt her blood pumping in her veins. She quickly came closer to them, put her big lips together, and, "*Umwah! Umwah! Umwah!*" it sounded like a plunger on the sink when she kissed each one on his head. Mother Monkey's warm breath was coming off her mouth. As she apologized, there was a sense of relief and a head nod among all monkeys that this was merely a misunderstanding and more food was brought.

Afterward, she turned toward the monkeys who were listening and watching what happened and said, "I am asking all of you to come with me and bring the food from the shore," Mother Monkey said then, "*Waaowa Jaooo*

Waaaa...!" Mother Monkey meant to say something like, "I expect you to behave, do not eat what you bring, just take it back..." she ordered them before they nodded their heads to express their obedience.

In no time, all monkeys started running behind Danilo who started walking fast with his dad and Andre toward the shore. Mother Monkey came along to supervise the transportation of the food to the colony.

This time it took the trio from Calape less than thirty minutes of a fast walk or a staggering run as the monkeys were walking fast and jumping in instances. They learned a lot about monkeys' life from this short journey. They learned that monkeys are very creative when it comes to getting their nutritional needs met.

Danilo, his dad, and Andre watched in amazement how the monkeys were drinking water from the streams or the mangroves. They do not use their tongue to lap the water up, they use their hand instead and make a cup. They watched some monkeys use large leaves and fold them to create a cup that they can drink out of.

When they arrived at the boat, some jumped on the boat to have fun, they'd never been on a boat.

As they were carrying the bags, "*Looo Jaooo Waaaa...Looo Jaooo Waaaa...!*" Mother Monkey meant to say something like, "I am repeating what I had told you before; do not eat, just take back...I am repeating what I had told you before; do not eat, just take back..." she angrily ordered them. All monkeys nodded their heads to show their obedience. They know not to upset their mom and know the consequences if she gets mad!

In the meantime, Danilo, Ernie, and Andre were busy splitting the fruit and fish boxes into several plastic bags so monkeys can easily carry them back.

After an hour or so, everyone was back in the colony loaded with food.

"I suggest you go back now as we have work to do. Our mission is already planned for tomorrow morning," Mother Monkey told Danilo, Ernie, and Andre.

"You can come back in a couple of days so I will let you know what happened," she ordered them to leave.

"Thank you, honorable Mother Monkey, see you in a couple of days," Ernie responded, Danilo and Andre, nodded their heads and waved goodbye.

On their way back to the boat, they seemed confused! Danilo pictured Mother Monkey running around the Hills, sniffing every tree, and identifying his missing friend. On the other hand, Ernie and Andre were very confused; they have no clue what she is doing or what she will be doing.

While on the boat going back to Calape, Andre leaned forward toward Ernie. He had an earnest look in his eyes.

"Can I ask you something?"

"Of course, *kapatid na lalaki* (a phrase that here means, 'Brother, you can ask anything. Say what's on your mind')," responded Ernie.

"*Salamat* Ernie! (this phrase means, thank you, Ernie!)" "Do you believe we are on the right track? Do you think that Mother Monkey will be able to bring my son back?"

"I remembered you've told me a few days ago something that I will never forget! You'd told me that at any given moment you have the power to say: This is not how the story is going to end. So, let's keep our faith alive my good friend!" Ernie's responded and gave Andre a big hug while holding on to the steering wheel. His eyes looked watery.

"Thank you, Ernie," Andre answered, leaned a little back, and went into deep silence. Meanwhile, in the colony, the monkeys stored the food in preparation for their big day.

One important aspect of monkeys' life is the fact that feeding is very crucial to their social life. When food is plentiful, they are usually timid and get along well within their groups. However, the lack of food creates a high level of stress for them.

After giving them a little rest, Mother Monkey howled, "*Chooooona*! Come on, it's time for training," she meant and quickly all adult monkeys came running from four different directions and lined behind their patrols' leaders.

"It is time for us to go and get as much as we can *Sampaguita 'Jasminium sambac'* flower. We need a lot of these flowers, as much as we can get! We will keep it in shade until tomorrow early morning. Each of you will be with her or his troop's leader. We will all be together, and we will take care of each other," Mother Monkey said and the monkeys nodded their heads.

Later on, they arrived in an area that is full of *Sampaguita* flowers. They began sniffing the flowers and picking them, and other monkeys were eating some of the flowers as they pick. All were happy; picking the flowers was fun!

The part of the area where they were picking the *Sampaguita* flowers is thick. The foliage of trees is very close to each other and forms a very thick canopy. In other parts, it is partially open and the sun shines all over it.

Regardless, it is a mossy green forest and a sea of deep green plant life. In the canopy, birds twittered and chirped while the monkeys were hearing a faint rustling of small rodents scampering through the foliage (foliage is a phrase that refers to when leaves, are collectively arranged by nature). They can hear the howling of a little fox. Over time, monkeys were taught how to survive, they know that there are some wild animals nearby.

In a few hours, they gathered a big load of the *Sampaguita* flowers and went back. "We will have the last drill after you eat your today's lunch. You will need to rest afterward as we will all get up very early as soon as we see the line of sunrise. I will explain more tomorrow," Mother Monkey instructed, reminded patrol leaders of their duties, and ordered everyone to go and eat.

It was an outstanding afternoon drill; Mother Monkey was happy with how they executed her plan during the mock mission. She ordered them to rest and be ready for the upcoming early morning. It was also the right time for her to rest.

Chapter Ten

Worried about the big day, Mother Monkey had woken up in the middle of the night. She was tossing and turning all night. She wasn't able to sleep. While the owl was hooting in the dark, she was thinking all night long about her plan. She wanted to make sure no mistakes will happen, she wants the safety of her family, and to ensure that her deception will keep the enemy off balance.

At this early time, she was feeling tired and got dark half-circles under her eyes due to her restless sleep.

"It is okay! I will sleep early today after we accomplish our mission!" she said as she was doing self-talk.

She got a clock ticking in her ear! Eager to ensure that the new day is an eclipse one, she stared at the sky, it was still dark. She waited and waited for a few hours to see whether the sun will come back. Now she started feeling comfortable the sun is on vacation.

As of now, the day in the colony was very different and the eclipse looks spectacular to watch. It was a full solar eclipse (known as a totality). Toady's day was almost as dark as the night.

Mother Monkey thought that the sun went on vacation and the moon is taking care of business in her absence.

"*Jawaaaa! Jawaaaa!*" Mother Monkey shouted in a loud voice that woke up everyone.

Mother Monkey probably meant to say something like, "Get up! Get up!"

She waited for almost ten minutes before all monkeys were up and getting ready for their big day. All monkeys were staring at the sun line, they figured out its absence. Mother Monkey asked all monkeys to eat first before giving them the complete plan for the day. As the food was brought in for them the day before, they were able to finish eating quickly. Today, they do not need to search for food.

As she noticed that all monkeys have done eating, "*Chooooona mama hopa!*" she meant to say, "Come on Mom, it's time for work!" Mother Monkey shouted.

Quickly all monkeys except the three babies and one mother ran toward the center of the colony and stood in lines of four patrols behind their leaders who stood intern behind Mother Monkey's Second in Command Leader.

"It's a big day for all of us. We are on a critical mission and I want you to carefully listen to me," Mother Monkey said.

Mother Monkey knows that walking freely in the Hills and sniffing for the scent of Carlo will be difficult unless ways can be found to defeat tarsiers' keen sense of smell. One way that she thought of is the use of flowers for masking scents that obscure her and her monkeys' family's familiar odors, making it less likely tarsiers will flee before she and her patrols can hunt Carlo.

"The smell is one of our most important survival mechanisms. If the Evil Giant or his allies can smell us, we will be in danger and will defeat our mission. We will need to conceal our scent, I want to smell nothing but *Sampaguita* coming from all of you," Mother Monkey continued her instructions.

"I order all of you to break and rub the *Sampaguita* flowers all over your palms and then wipe its juice all over your face and your full body. Make sure to apply a generous amount of the flower," she continued and started breaking the *Sampaguita* flowers and rubbing them all over her body and face. All monkeys were nodding their heads, breaking, and rubbing the flower. They all smell as if they just had a *Sampaguita's* flower bath.

"This is perfect! I also want you to take the leftover with you, you can throw the leftover flowers on the ground of the Hills upon arrival," she said.

"Let's sniff the boy's clothes for the last time," she said and passed Carlo's clothes for all to sniff.

"One more thing, I want you to take as much food as you could and eat when you get hungry. Very importantly, you will keep up with your patrol and follow their lead and instructions, with no deviation whatsoever. Is it clear?" Mother Monkey asked, then all nodded their heads up and down, meaning 'yes!'

"The Evil Giant of the Hills is a giant creature having the forms of various animals in combination, my ancestors described him as a Griffin, some call him Griffon or Gryphon, is a creature with the body, tail, and back legs of a lion and a head and wings of an eagle. Sometimes, he has an eagle's talons as its front feet. During this time of the eclipse, the Evil Giant will be weak as he gets his energy only from the light of the sun and regards the eclipse as a bad omen," Mother Monkey described him and continued her assurance by saying, "Other animals are scared of him and support him out of fear. However, we will not go if I felt that your lives will be endangered."

The monkeys were listening and watching in amazement at the unusual light as the disk of the Sun is fully obscured by the Moon. The colony and its surroundings are mostly brilliantly illuminated, with only a small dark patch showing the Moon's shadow.

"Are you scared?" she asked.

"No, we are not scared!" they screamed back.

"I love you all! Let's go! We will need to be careful as it will be dark in the jungle and we might face some wild animals on our long journey to the Hills!" Mother Monkey ordered.

In no time, the monkeys started their journey in the calm jungle as the early morning was mostly overcast. They can rarely hear the morning birds chirp; they seem as if they too were on vacation away. On their way, they can see and sense the many animals that still running around. They have to be careful and, in some instances, adult monkeys needed to chase them away and they all needed to run away. All monkeys were using all of their five senses to stay away from danger. This is the nature of their life; they call it survival! The road was also full of tall bamboo sticks and entangled trees with wet, muddy leaves. This journey is hard as they tried to avoid the swamps to keep the scent of the flowers alive.

"You will need to be careful, not to get muddy or wet. You need to preserve the *Sampaguita's* flower smell for now!" Mother Monkey said.

After a long walk in the dark jungle, they now can see the Chocolate Hills in the dark. "Wow! Here we are," one of the monkeys shouted.

"Patrol leaders, it's time for you to move as planned, Northeast, Southeast, Northwest, and Southwest. I will enter from the East and our Second Command Leader from the West. When inside, we will all start the rituals and sniffing of all dark hollows that are close to the ground or near the trees' trunks. Whoever finds the tree that matches the scent of the boy must immediately tell her or his patrol leader to validate and finish the job as the patrol leader is older, stronger, and knows how to carry the tarsier out of the Hills!" Mother Monkey instructed.

"Are we ready?" she asked.

"Yes, Mother Monkey, we are ready!" they shouted and started running behind the patrol leaders to enter the Hills. After almost half an hour, all monkeys reached their assigned spots (Northeast, Northwest, Southeast, and Southwest) and singled to Mother Monkey and Second Command Leader their readiness to enter their assigned area of the forest.

"Jomaaaa Owoo!" that phrase possibly meant, "Go ahead and enter the forest," which was a loud vocalizing sound that came out from Mother Monkey signaling her approval to enter the Hills.

"*Hogaa! Hogaa! Hogaa! Hogaa!*" the phrase *Hogaa* was only used by the monkeys just to confuse others in the Hills, it has no actual meaning to them or others.

They entered the Hills from four different directions. All monkeys were chanting, dancing, and raising their hands and heads toward the sun in well-practiced choreographic movements. Some monkeys were spreading *Sampaguita* to the ground, near the trunks or the hollows of the trees while sniffing for Carlo's scent. In the meantime, all tarsiers ran up to their trees. Tarsiers felt safe as the monkeys seemed to be peaceful, funny, smiling, entertaining, and friendly, and they smelled nice.

Suddenly, trees started shaking, some branches and leaves started falling off the trees, and a loud, yet ailing voice roared through the Hills.

"Who are you, *Sampaguita's* monkeys? You smell very different than the monkeys I got to know; I have never met your monkey type before! What are you doing here in my Kingdom on this day stupid, *Sampaguita* monkeys?" It was the Evil Giant's voice, no one can see how he looked.

Some of the monkeys became scared and trembling, they had never heard of voices like that. However, their patrol leaders are strong, well-trained, and know how to motivate other monkeys. They quickly shouted at their monkeys' brothers and sisters saying, "Be brave like all of us, no need to be afraid! We are very strong! Keep chanting!"

Quickly, another loud voice came, "We are a special breed of monkeys, and we smell *Sampaguita* and are named *Sampaguita* monkeys simply because *Sampaguita* is our usual diet. We are here to give our respect and obedience to Your Highness King of the Hills! ('Highness' is a title used to address or refer to a royal person) We have been instructed by our ancestors to come when we can and bring to your Highness our rituals and flowers to ward off nasty evil spirits or bad luck," it was the voice of Mother Monkey.

"I know you do not feel good today, this is why we are here to wish you well and offer our loyalty! Your health is very important to me and to

Sampaguita monkeys' family, we want to see you getting better," she continued deceiving him.

Mother Monkey usually is honest and does not like deceiving others. Today she seemed to have no other choice but to do so to save her family and Carlo.

"I understand the reason why you are here! But, eating only *Sampaguita* is something I do not understand! What would you eat during the dry season when no *Sampaguita* can be found?" he questioned her.

"We usually store *Sampaguita* in tree holes to eat during the dry season. However, we will eat twigs and dry bark if we don't find other flowers as we need to survive. We also eat sap; this is a good nutritious for us (sap is the blood or liquid of a tree. It carries energy out into the branches when new buds are forming in springtime). We need to survive, Your Highness," she replied.

"Ha! Ha! Ha! Now, I got it! I had never met your monkey type before. Meeting and having you in the Hills will be a good addition to my army!" he said.

"It will be our utmost pleasure to serve, Your Highness!" she replied.

"But…Who told you that I am ill?" asked the Evil Giant.

"It was one of your loyal foxes who dropped by my colony in the early morning to tell me the bad news. I was saddened to hear such news," Mother Monkey said. "I became a good friend of this fox over time, we live close by," Mother Monkey added.

"Ha! Ha! Ha! Foxes are very smart, they can always tell when I am sick, and when I am healthy! I am happy to know that! Yes, my dear flower-smelling monkey, I am ill and very weak today. I will be very strong tomorrow!" the Evil Giant asserted.

"I am very happy to hear that! No…No…I meant to say, I will be very happy when I know that you are healthy!" said Mother Monkey and added, "On behalf of all the *Sampaguita's* monkeys, we wish Your Highness King of the Hills a speedy recovery! We will continue our rituals to keep the bad evils away from you, away from your Kingdom, and away from your trees!" she signaled to all monkeys to continue their rituals, performing their crazy dance, spreading some *Sampaguita* on the ground, and continuing the search for Carlo by sniffing the trees.

The sniffing mission was not that easy when you had already rubbed your body with *Sampaguita* flower, monkeys needed to sniff harder and be more careful to recognize the right scent. Doing so was taking more time than expected.

"This is good, but let me tell you that you and your flowers' monkeys are fools for doing these stupid rituals!" the Evil Giant suggested.

"Am I a fool? I will soon show you who is a fool!" Mother Monkey mumbled, then said in a loud voice, "Of course, we are fools, Your Highness! You are the only intelligent being, this is why we are here to serve and obey you!"

The Giant Evil became more conceded and said, "Very well! I will order you to come back tomorrow so you and your stupid monkeys will join my army."

"We would love to do so as it would be a great honor to be a part of your influential Kingdom, Your Highness!" Mother Monkey replied with a big smile as the monkeys were performing their crazy rituals of, "*Hogaa! Hogaa! Hogaa! Hogaa!*"

Suddenly, it was time for one of the patrol's leaders to quickly come closer to a particular tree, it was apparent that one of the monkeys was able to identify the right tree and asked his patrol leader to validate and capture the tarsier. In no time, Mother Monkey quickly came closer to that same tree, sniffed it, and sniffed the tarsier who was clanged to his tree and ordered the patrol's leader to quickly capture the tarsier.

The monkey patrol leader quickly climbed the tree, grabbed the tarsier, and screamed, "Let's go!" Quickly, all monkeys ran in one direction following their leaders. Mother Monkey and her Second Command Leader were running behind them to ensure all are safe.

As they were running out, "Voowaa…Voowaa…!" probably, she meant to say something like, "Hurry up…hurry up…" Mother Monkey called, and a strangely deep, yet still ailing voice thundered through the Hills and silenced her call.

"What do you want and what are you doing here? It is me again, the King of the Hills! Get on your knees for me and beg me forgiveness for what you have done!" the Evil Giant of the Hills screamed and started throwing some tree branches and rocks at the monkeys.

As they were running out, branches were getting in their way and on their faces and creating some injuries.

"Get on my knees and ask for your forgiveness? Ha…Ha…Ha…! You are arrogant, yet a stupid Evil, I will not even bother to think about it!" replied Mother Monkey.

"Did you call me stupid?" he asked.

"Yes, I did say that to Your Miserable Evil of the Hills!" Mother Monkey mocked him.

"What fate brings you here when I am ill? Now I know who you are! You are the same monkey who had managed to come last time when I was ill too. I will soon get to punish you and your little weak army of monkeys. I will punish you as soon as I get back my usual superpower! No one…I mean no one, will escape my punishment!" the Evil Giant sounded while in an angry mood and voice. "You'll need to fear me!" the Evil Giant added.

"Today, you are ill, no followers support you, and no power! Why should I be scared of you, you fool evil?" Mother Monkey asserted.

"Listen to me, stupid monkey! Are you making fun of me by calling me a fool? I vow…never…never…never…to rest before I get you!" he was screaming in anger!

"I will have no compromise and no sympathy for you or your monkeys. There's no kindness if you're against the Giant King of the Hills…I am the sole King here; you'll soon pay dearly!" his voice was suffocated by anger and hate toward her.

"Ha…Ha…Ha…" Mother Monkey laughed loudly, it's strange how much joy she got from the Evil Giant's agony.

"Are you mocking me now, your stupid flower monkey?" he asked her while annoyed. "Yes, I am! I will tell the jungle animals to laugh at your stupidity! Enjoy your miserable day, stupid Evil!" she said as she approached the end of the Hills, she was bursting with joy.

In the meantime, tarsier Carlo was very frightened! Similar to what happened to Danilo before; he started resisting being captured and biting the capturing monkey. He unsuccessfully asked for help from other tarsiers and the Evil Giant by sending ultrasonic sounds. The Giant Evil and other tarsiers were still in shock! The monkey patrol leader who captured tarsier Carlo is very strong, he held him by wrapping one of his feet around it as Mother Monkey instructed him.

In the meantime, tarsier Carlo continued unsuccessfully fighting his way to escape. Finally, Mother Monkey asked everyone to stop as they reached the safe territory. Then, she brought some wild plants' vines and tied the tarsier's hands, legs, and tail like she did previously with tarsier Danilo. She does not want him to run away.

"It is time for you to rest and eat. I want to congratulate all of you on a successful and brave mission, we have indeed accomplished all that we wanted to accomplish. Very importantly, I am delighted that none of us got seriously injured from the falling trees' branches," Mother Monkey asserted as the monkeys cheered her.

At this moment, all monkeys were very happy, they used their facial expressions to display their pride, sense of their achievements, and feelings for one another. Mother Monkey and other leaders were busy hugging their patrol members, putting wet leaves on the minor cuts of some injured monkeys, and cuddling with them like babies. All monkeys were laughing at how they deceived the Evil Giant and how Mother Monkey made fun of him.

After a little while, tarsier Carlo started feeling a little at ease as the monkeys played and cuddled with him. They collected some insects and gave them to Carlo so he can eat them. Tarsier Carlo felt a little comfortable but confused. The monkeys started treating him as if he is one of them.

Tired and did not sleep well, Mother Monkey laid down for a little bit on the ground to rest, and then, "We had sniffed many tarsiers to find the boy, are there any more humans there?" she uttered aloud in anguish.

"It is time to leave the area before it gets too late and more dangerous," Mother Monkey asserted. "We will need to be super careful as we might encounter some wild animals or snakes. While we are going together, each monkey must follow her or his patrol leader,"

Mother Monkey ordered before all monkeys obeyed her order and walked behind their patrols leaders on their way back to the colony.

Chapter Eleven

It was a very dark evening when Mother Monkey and her troop got back to their territory. Once inside the colony, she can't ignore but notice the trio from Calape. She can still recognize them in the dark from a distance. They were sitting and seemed like three rocks until they stood up and looked like three dwarf trees in the dark.

As the trio hear the monkeys coming, Ernie flashed his flashlight toward them. The monkeys got scared and surprised at first, they have not seen a flashlight before.

As they got a little closer, Mother Monkey stared at the flashlight, rubbing her eyebrow furiously. "So," she finally said, "What are you doing here and how did you get that *baby sun* with you?" she uttered and referred to the flashlight as a *baby sun.*

"How did you get the baby of the sun? Did the sun go out today to deliver her baby?" she asked. And when she finished her question, she held her breath, waiting for him to explain.

"No," Ernie said cautiously. "This has nothing to do with the sun, it is just a light," Ernie answered, he had a grin on his face. He never expected that question.

Then, Mother Monkey added, "Let me see it," Mother Monkey held the flashlight and started flashing everywhere. And, *"Wahoo...Wahoo...!"* Mother Monkey meant to say something like, *"Wow...wow...!* You must be connected to spirits!" she said.

"You'll need to return the baby sun to his mother regardless. This is not fair to the mother or the baby!" Mother Monkey demanded.

"I'll do so, Mother Monkey, as soon as I go back to my hometown," Ernie responded that way as he felt it was difficult for him to reason or to explain what a flashlight is, she had never been exposed to it.

It was dark and damp, everyone was staring at the tarsier who is supposed to be Carlo. However, there was no evidence to suggest that the tarsier she brought in is Carlo. Flashing the light on the tarsier showed a mixed flash of fear and apprehension clouding his face as he hastily eyed Danilo, Ernie, and Andre. Everyone there appeared very emotional! Tarsier's Carlo couldn't resist keeping his eyes off Danilo's face as if he wanted to tell him something. That simple gesture affected Danilo deeply, his tears were running down his face like a waterfall coming down from a steep fall over a rocky ledge. Danilo was feeling bad and sorry while in a complete state of fear.

Danilo wasn't able to hold back his emotions — he started sobbing and his tears were flowing like a little water fountain. This tarsier brought him a back flash. Danilo recalled the time when he entered the Hills with Carlo and was surrounded by tarsiers. He can remember the piercing noise that came from inside the hills. He still remembers being surrounded by the hundreds of chirping tarsiers hopping on the ground like frogs. He can also remember them being scared and screaming at them to no one who could've come and helped. The scene of the changes to Carlo's body and face from a human being to a tarsier quickly came to Danilo's mind.

As he stared at the tarsier, the feeling of the bond to that particular being was controlling his mind, that bond is still living in him and never waned.

"You better stay away from the tarsier, I do not want him to be afraid," Mother Monkey told Danilo, Ernie, and Andre.

"I have to do something very important now," she added, then carried the tarsier and left to the seashore. She wanted to bathe him as she did before when she brought back Danilo as a tarsier from the Hills. She wanted him to be purified and knows it will take some time. Like the experience Danilo had with moonlighting bathing, tarsier Carlo was also unaware of what and why she was doing what she does.

Meanwhile, it is too late and too dark to go back to Calape. The trio decided to spend the night in the colony. Their families in Calape anticipated they do spend the night in the colony. For them to sleep there, it will be prudent to have a little fire to keep animals away. They started collecting dry branches to start the fire. Important to note that starting a fire in the jungle could be very dangerous if someone does not know how. Ernie and Andre built a safe fire in an area away from the trees or dried grass or bushes. Additionally, they've made a circle of rocks around it to prevent the fire from going outside.

The fire brought life to the colony as darkness wriggled over the wet ground. The colony is surrounded by the sounds of many animals who inhabited the nearby area. As the dark makes a more serene colony; the sounds of the frogs croaking, the wolves howling, the owls hooting, the coyotes growling and huffing, and other animals' noises from a distance made it an adventure for the Calape's trio.

The monkeys came running to the fire, showing no signs of the fear that other animals normally exhibit. Instead, they were happily performing a ritualistic fire dance while facing the flames. They were very happy at the scene of the fire.

Upon coming back from the waterfront, Mother Monkey was happy to see others having a good time. She avoided bringing the tarsier closer to the fire as she believes he will be scared.

In the meantime, Andre was impatiently waiting for her return. As soon as he spotted her, he ran closer to her and flashed his light to see the supposedly his tarsier's son, but Mother Monkey quickly reacted and started shrieking.

"Janoosa…Janoosa!" probably meant to say, "Stay away…Stay away!" Mother Monkey shouted so loud you could have heard her from a faraway distance.

"I warned you not to scare him – do not get the baby sun closer to him *Janoosa*!" Mother Monkey asserted and let the tarsier goes up the tree. She was deeply hurt and upset!

Andre nodded. "Sorry, Mother Monkey, I don't mean to get you upset!"

"Insisting on seeing him and upsetting Mother Monkey won't get me back anything otherwise. Let me just listen and obey her, I have no other choice," Andre mumbled and walked back to the fire site.

Upon his arrival, he told Ernie of what had happened and ended the story by saying, "Although she is a good soul, she has a bad attitude!"

Ernie smiled. "Don't dwell on what Mother Monkey did, my friend Andre. We don't have any choice…We need to wait and make sure that the captured tarsier is Carlo!"

"I just hope he is—" Andre started to say, but then his lips compressed with the effort to hold back what he was thinking, he looked away and started weeping.

"Be strong, my good friend, keep up your hope alive," Ernie said and gave him a big hug.

In a few minutes, Mother Monkey came down to sit closer to the fire, she sat between Ernie and Andre and tossed her arm over Andre's shoulder to demonstrate friendship and trust through connectivity, she knew she hurt his feelings. Andre and Ernie reciprocated by tossing their arms over her shoulders. Everyone felt good and continued watching the monkeys dancing and being in a joyful mood! These monkeys were so humorous, versatile (the word versatile meant they have the desire to show off, they wanted to try everything), and sociable. They got along well with Andre, Danilo, and Ernie. They wanted to dance with them so the trio from Calape danced with them to their laughing.

Spending some time in the colony, the trio from Calape quickly noticed and learned that these funny and loving monkeys were competitive too, they like to compete with each other and show they are better dancers than others. They also are gifted and learned quickly from each other; they were lots of fun!

Contrary to this, these monkeys love playing and hate restraints. Additionally, they lack patience, perseverance (this is another word to describe someone's ability and self-control that pushes her/him to work through challenges), and responsibility, and they are short-sighted (this term meant to say that they are ill-judged about things). Moreover, they are showing excessive pride and self-satisfaction in their achievements or abilities, and are not down-to-earth.

Monkey males are competitive and vain (meaning that they have an excessively high opinion of one's appearance and ability). They look mysterious and untrammeled (a term to mean that a male monkey is not deprived of freedom of action or expression). They are also careless, sloppy, and volatile. Opposite to them is the female monkeys who are usually smart and easy-going. They are beautiful, sociable, charming, entertaining, and interesting. However, they are moody, impatient, cunning, and conceited. Mother Monkey is no different.

It was toward the middle of the night when the monkeys were exhausted and started going to sleep.

"The kids are tired," Mother Monkey said, her eyes shining. "As they got up very early and worked hard, they need a good night's sleep," Mother Monkey added and left the fire area, she was very exhausted as she did not sleep the night before.

The trio from Calape nodded their heads and said goodnight. They lay down closer to the fire, trying to rest. The night was so quiet, that they can only hear the howling of the nearby foxes and other animals' noises. Just for more safety, they collected lots of dry wigs to add to the fire as needed for them to scare animals away.

While they were so tired, it was difficult for them to sleep. They were up almost all night watching from a faraway and watching as much as they can see in the dark the supposedly Carlo as they know that tarsiers become active at night. The supposed-to-be tarsier Carlo was hunting bats, frogs, grasshoppers, beetles, lizards, and other insects. He seemed hungry. While on the ground, he hopped like a frog and moved with a quadrupedal walk. He was moving back and forth to the tree branch. He goes down to the ground for just a few moments while trapping and eating an insect before returning to the tree. The tarsier was staring at them when he is on the tree, yet seemed surprised and afraid of the fire.

The trio from Calape was watching in an emotional state. Danilo was imagining himself doing that as a tarsier while feeling bad for Carlo. On the other hand, Ernie was so sad watching the tarsier, feeling bad for Carlo, and imagining what his son went through. In the meantime, Andre was in disbelief and tears as he was watching. In a little while, the trio closed their eyes trying to sleep. Sleeping in the colony reminded Danilo of the time when he was living there with the monkeys while waiting for someone to take him back to his family.

On the next day, the colony was silent when Danilo woke up in the early morning with a dull headache. It was still dark, but he got up as he was not able to sleep. No one was awake yet, he walked around and was able to spot tarsier Carlo clanging to a tree. He wanted to check on him to see if he can recognize him. Standing a few feet away from the tree, the tarsier couldn't move his eyes away from Danilo as if he knows him and wanted to say something. At then, Danilo was a little scared, his imagination of himself being a tarsier came quickly back. He quickly returned to the spot where his dad and Andre were sleeping, he does not want anyone to see him close to Carlo. He knows that Mother Monkey will get easily upset.

In a little while, it was getting to be a beautiful morning. The sun shed its golden reflection on the wildflowers that were dotting the colony and the beyond fields. The branches in the colony were hanging down low, dropping leaves now and then. The sky was cloudless and vibrant. The colony seemed very peaceful; nothing interrupted the silence but the sound of the softly running water from the nearby creek. The colony seemed less terrifying than when it was clouded with darkness.

Danilo can easily see the running wolf from a short distance, this is the first time he sees a wolf. He wasn't scared at all, knowing that the wolf will not come closer as he knows that this is the monkeys' territory and that he will be in danger if he does so. The wolf seemed a little frightened as the body looked small and less conspicuous. The ears were flattened down against the head and the tail was tucked between the legs. The wolf was whimpering (a phrase that meant that the wolf was making a series of low, feeble 'cries' sounds expressive of fear).

Over the time spent in the colony, Danilo continued learning more about animals. Wolves, monkeys, and other animals are very smart beings – they know where what, and who they should avoid. They have reasoning capabilities. Observing them, was a good experiential learning lesson for him.

Ernie and Andre just woke up and slowly the three of them walked across the colony toward the tree where the tarsier was to get a glimpse at what they suspect is Carlo. The tarsier was quietly clinging vertically to the tree branch. As he noticed them staring at him from a distance, he acted shy and nervous. They can easily tell that he has large, sensitive ears to detect even the smallest of sounds. All were teared up, they can sense and hear each other's groan (a phrase which means here a low-pitched cry of grief).

"I wish he can talk to me!" Danilo said while sobbing quietly.

"Hush! Let's leave quickly before Mother Monkey sees us, we cannot afford to agitate her," Andre said and rushed away as Ernie and Danilo quickly followed.

They went down the little hill to drink from the nearby creek. They took with them the leftover food they brought with them the day before and started eating on the way, everyone was hungry. Upon drinking, they took a short resting by the creek. Everyone and everything around was quiet except for the sounds of the soft murmur of the creek water and the chirping of the birds. As the sun was pouring through, the creek seemed more beautiful because they got to hope that they might see Carlo soon!

"Today, we must go back home and be with our family. Our family is worried and waiting for news. Additionally, Mother Monkey does not want us here," suggested Ernie.

"I agree my friend! Let's initiate our departure and ask Mother Monkey when we come back," Andre responded.

"How about collecting some flowers and give to her when she gets up to show her our appreciation?" Danilo suggested.

"It is a great idea, let's do it fast," responded Ernie as Andre nodded.

In and around the colony, there are many varieties of wildflowers and it can be hard to pick just one. In a matter of no time, the trio collected lots of different flowers, and trimmed the stems, while being careful to leave just enough that gives the flower a hint of green.

"Now what is next?" asked Danilo.

"Let's be creative with what we have here," Andre suggested and started getting some leaves.

A few minutes later, they carefully added to the flowers some beautiful tree leaves, tied it all together with wild plants' vines to make it look like a beautiful bouquet, and waited for Mother Monkey to wake up.

In a little while, the monkeys started getting up and roaming around (a phrase which means here, they were moving or wandering in an aimless, ambling, unrestricted manner around) looking for food. It is time for them to eat. Some came closer to play with Danilo and others were trying to catch the flower arrangement thinking it is food. Ernie tried his best to keep it away from them until Mother Monkey suddenly woke up, she rolled her eyes, and then, "Bloom… Bloom… Tchawaaa… Waaa… Waaa," which probably meant something along the lines of "I am upset…I am upset, what you are doing is embarrassing!" the corner of her mouth quirked up (a phrase which meant, she was showing her disapproval or expressing her disgust with what the monkeys were doing).

She screamed at the monkeys to stop chasing Ernie.

Then, "Come in closer." She stood up and asked the three of them to get closer to her. "This is a beautiful arrangement, who is this for?" Mother Monkey asked.

"It is our way to say thank you for what you have done for us! You are a great leader!" Ernie told her.

"You are a wonderful person!" added Andre as Danilo quickly got closer to hug her.

"I am so happy and delighted that you appreciate me!" Mother Monkey said, her eyes filing up with tears. All nodded and gave her a big hug coupled with a big smile.

"I'm sorry, sir," Mother Monkey told Andre. "I may have been harsh with you recently when I didn't intend to be. It was so difficult for me to accommodate your desire to be closer to your son while I want to make sure that your son is safe and not scared." She glanced toward the tarsier, and tears welled in her eyes. Afterward, she quickly opened and closed her mouth, which caused her lips to smack together and make a noise. It is the monkeys' way of apologizing and making sure all is forgiven.

"I understand and no worries at all, you are a good mother, and we very much appreciate you," replied Andre.

"Um…Um…Mother Monkey, it is time for us to go home…Um, for now, we will go home and we will be back to your colony as soon as you want us to be back," said Danilo.

"Uh…That is good! Have a safe trip and won't be back before ten sunrises (she meant to say after ten days)."

"Okay, Mother Monkey, we will see you after ten sunrises," Danilo answered back and gave her and the other monkeys hugs and kisses. Ernie and Andre nodded and shook her hand and waved to other monkeys before the three walked away from the colony toward the shore to go home.

After their leaving, Mother Monkey sat down quietly on her tree stump thinking and doing self-talk.

"I am very happy with what I have done. I am also happy with their token of appreciation for what my family and I have done. I should be thankful to the Wise Monkey for his wisdom and care, I should take this beautiful flower arrangement and give it to him instead. He is more deserving!"

Quickly, Mother Monkey shouted at her patrol leaders, "*Chooooona mama hopona!*" she meant to say, "Come on to me, Mom needs you!" Mother Monkey shouted.

In no time, patrol leaders came, stood around her, and listened to what she wanted to say, "I need you to take care of everyone, I am going to deliver this present 'the flower arrangement' to the Wise Monkey. He indeed was greatly wise! I will be back as soon as I can," Mother Monkey said, and she hugged them all before saying goodbye.

Mother Monkey knows that she always needs to be careful walking in the jungle, the memory of her losing her husband is still fresh in her mind and will continue to be. She needs to come back before dark. She was trying to overcome her sorrow by being good to her family members and through helping others and saving the lives of Danilo and Carlo. She was carefully walking and sometimes running on the wet grass and moss. She was wondering how the Wise Monkey will react upon receiving the beautiful flower arrangement.

"I think, he will be cheerful and thankful to me for bringing it to him!"

"Not exactly," she corrected herself and said, "I think he will tell me that I have made him feel like the King of the forest today…He will be so happy when I show him the flower arrangement. I also believe he will thank me for the time and thoughts I put into giving him such a wonderful gift…Mother

Monkey, you are the best." Mother Monkey kept using her imagination, entertaining herself, and doing her self-talk while watching her way through the forest.

Upon her arrival, the Wise Monkey was sitting on his tree stump, surrounded by his staff discussing matters. Quickly, he stood up to welcome her by saying, "I am happy to see you again, Mother Monkey, please come closer to me!" As she came closer to the Wise Monkey and his staff, the Wise Monkey walked toward her as she gestured to him that the flower arrangement is for him.

"This is very kind of you, Mother Monkey…This is a wonderful gift that made my day! You are very kind and thoughtful, I very much appreciate your quality!" the Wise Monkey said while Mother Monkey's face turned red. She was very happy that he liked the gift, however, she was shy.

"I was wondering what happened yesterday and how did it go?" asked the Wise Monkey.

"It was fabulous!" Mother Monkey answered and told him in detail exactly what had happened.

As soon as she finished telling him the story, "Ha…Ha…Ha…you are incredible, this is amazingly smart and funny." The Wise Monkey along with everyone present engaged in a belly laugh (a phrase to mean here, a loud deep laugh). You can hear them laughing from a faraway distance.

"I am here to thank you for your advice. If it wasn't for you, I wouldn't be successful!" Mother Monkey responded.

The Wise Monkey blinked and took a deep breath, then grinned. "Sorry!" he smiled and closed his eyes for brief seconds. "Not at all, Mother Monkey, advice alone is not enough! The plan and its execution are very important! You are very impressive and I am very proud of your intelligence and leadership," the Wise Monkey added before he ordered one of his assistants to bring her a special recognition award.

A few minutes later, his assistant came back and gave him a wood log that the Wise Monkey himself had engraved with the face of a laughing monkey. The Wise Monkey hugged Mother Monkey, handed her the wooden log, and said, "Please accept this award as a symbol of recognizing your courage and commitment to help others and save lives! I am very proud to know you…You are a remarkable mother!"

Upon receiving the award, Mother Monkey was overwhelmed with happiness, love, and appreciation for what she did. She shrieked loudly and gasped for air before completely going numb and falling to her knees. Her lips trembled as she cried and her eyes were filled to the brim with tears. She couldn't do anything other than cry. This award and his words just made her break down crying happy tears.

Flushed with excitement, "Thank you, Honorable Wise Monkey, I am humbled by what you did and said!" She couldn't control her emotions. Mother Monkey cried tears of happiness as she felt that she was on cloud nine (cloud nine is an idiom that means here that she felt that she was in seventh heaven or on top of the world).

They looked at each other for a few seconds, and then they laughed. However, her laugh stuck in her throat when glanced at the Wise Monkey and saw him pleasant and happy. And just at that moment, Mother Monkey glanced her way out saying, "It is already getting late, and need to keep going before it gets dark before I arrive there," she excused herself. Mother Monkey wanted to stay there longer as she was happy being in the presence of the Wise Monkey, however, she needs to get back to the colony before it gets dark.

"Have a safe trip, Honorable Mother Monkey, and please come by at any time!" replied the Wise Monkey. Then he leaned over Mother Monkey, putting a hand gently on her stiff shoulder.

"I'll do anything to help you, Honorable Mother Monkey," the Wise Monkey whispered as she grabbed her award and happily made her way outside his colony. She was contented, there was one thing she was confident of and that is, that Wise Monkey appreciated her and will do anything he could to help her.

Chapter Twelve

Even though it was nearly sunset when arrived back at the colony, Mother Monkey was done being scared. Her conversations with the Wise Monkey gave her the needed strength and confidence. Upon arrival, all the monkeys rushed to greet her and were amazed to listen to her story and see the recognition award.

Afterward, "This award is for all of us, not only me! All of you had enormously contributed to the success of what we did yesterday. I am very proud of you all," Mother Monkey addressed her colony members and then all danced in celebration.

In the meantime, the trio from Calape had already gotten home earlier than expected. They arrived home around 10:00 in the morning. As luck would have it, there wasn't a cloud in the sky, and Ernie had no problem navigating his fishing boat. At their homes, family members were anxiously waiting for their arrival with hope.

"Where is my son?" Sonia, Carlo's mom, asked in a frenzy way. She was in extreme mental agitation. Carlo's siblings and grandparents were crying too. They were in despair as soon as they notice Andre getting inside the house alone. Quickly, Andre calmed his family down, explained to them in detail what happened, and urged them to be patient. The same thing happened with Cora (Danilo's mom). While she was happy to see her husband and son back, "Did you bring back Carlo?" Cora franticly asked and Ernie and Danilo told her exactly what happened.

On the same day in the mid-afternoon, Danilo asked his parents if he can go to see Paco. Ernie accompanied him to the Banana shore and waited together to see the dolphin. However, Paco did not show up on this day.

"Don't worry, he already left. We will go back next weekend," Ernie assured Danilo.

"I understand, hope to see him soon! I missed him dearly!" Danilo walked back home with his dad; he was a little sad that he did not see his dolphin friend.

Back in the colony, Mother Monkey watched the tarsier starting his day at sunset trapping and eating insects, beetles, and lizards. She quickly left him some fish under his tree that he hesitantly ate. Later on, Mother Monkey grabbed him and took him for his daily ritual of bathing in the sea under the moonlight. It took the tarsier almost three days to feel comfortable with other monkeys and started having a fun time playing with them.

Mother monkey continued bathing the tarsier nightly for over a week and like Danilo when he was a tarsier, changes started taking effect on his face and body. His eyes and ears became smaller, his tail unexpectedly disappeared, and his hands, fingers, and legs started changing shape too. She kept bathing him in the sea under the light of the moon until amazingly one night, he turned back into a real boy. He turned back to his original Carlo and started swimming for a short period.

Like his friend Danilo, he was purified!

Still not fully conscious, he was confused and does not know or recall anything. His mind was still absent! He went back to play with the monkeys and eat his meal.

After a couple of days, he saw Mother Monkey and remembered her. He was scared and in a state of disbelief. He tried unsuccessfully running away from her, he recalled her being the same monkey that he and Danilo had encountered on the coconut farm.

"Where's Danilo?" an agonized Carlo asked while crying his eyes out.

"He is safe, you do not have to worry about him at all! He is coming back after one or two sunrises. I saved you from the Evil Giant of the Hills. Carlo does not remember anything other than the fact of him seeing Danilo changing into a tarsier."

"It is complicated!" Mother Monkey told him and asked him to be patient until Danilo and his dad come to pick him up.

"You have been in our colony for over nine sunrises (9 days). You have now purified from being a tarsier and been liberated from serving the Evil Giant of the Hills," Mother Monkey told frightened, yet confused Carlo. He still does not know exactly what happened to him and for how long he was going through this. It seemed like a nightmare!

"Is Danilo okay?" he anxiously asked her again.

"Yes, he is. You will soon see him," she assured him.

"How about my family?" he asked again.

"Your dad will soon arrive with Danilo. Just give them one or two sunrises to come," she responded and then took him back to the colony.

An apprehended Carlo returned to the colony with Mother Monkey. He sat down beneath a tree and cried. He was not in the mood to eat.

Later, heavy clouds hang over the colony and steady rain started falling. Some monkeys hid under trees watching others playing in the rain and some came to play with Carlo who was sadly quiet and in tears. Mother Monkey gave him the clothes his dad brought the other day to wear.

Like other monkeys, Carlo hid under dense foliage to protect himself from the rain. He was still in shock, confused, and not able to comprehend what happened. The ground was still muddy from the rain, but he sat down regardless. He has nowhere to go. As the rainy night enfolded the colony, Carlo was worried, he couldn't sleep the whole night. He was not sure when his dad or someone else will be able to find him as he is in the middle of nowhere, and he does not know where exactly he was.

He was never sure about what Mother Monkey had said, he is so scared of her. He believes that she is mean, she did something bad to Danilo, she had a bad intention, and she had something to do with keeping him here.

"Maybe, I should run away!" Danilo was doing self-talk. "Where to? It is scary out there and I might face the wild animals that I hear about all time. But…" Then, "I think the monkeys are nice to me, they will not hurt me. Let me wait for a little bit." Carlo kept thinking. "If Mother Monkey wants to hurt me, she could have already done it. Maybe she is kind but this is how she acts. She acts that way with her own family, then she hugged them."

On the second day, it was still raining cats and dogs (an idiom to mean it was heavy rain). He can see the cascades of rain everywhere in and around the colony. The dark sky was lit up by lightning. Lightning flashed across the sky. In the meantime, all monkeys were sleeping, they are used to sleeping during different types of weather. Carlo was alone and scared of the storms, besides he was anxious to see his family and his friend.

At the same time, it was early morning in Calape. Andre, Danilo, and Ernie were getting ready to go back to the colony with the hope to bring Carlo home. It is a big day for them and their families! After the light showers during the night, it began to storm and rain in earnest in the early morning. The morning looked different; the high sunlit clouds drifted across a clear blue sky. Ernie knows firsthand that sailing in such weather is a bad idea. Ernie's small boat is not equipped for this weather.

Worried about a risky trip, Ernie had trouble thinking. He was watching the pouring rain outside through the sole window of his little living room and hearing the noise of the stubborn winds; he can hear the rumbling in the distance. As a fisherman, he can predict how the weather will look in the upcoming hours. Ernie sighed then, "Let's wait for a little more time, *mahal na kaibigan* (a term to mean 'dear friend' in the local language), it is risky to sail that far in this stormy and rainy weather," Ernie told Andre. "We will face an abnormal rise in seawater level during a storm like this."

"I understand, *kapatid na lalaki* (a phrase that here means 'Brother')," responded a despaired Andre, his eyes flooded with tears. At that time, Danilo kept quiet as tears filled his eyes. Meanwhile, Cora was in the kitchen preparing coffee and breakfast while hiding away her tears.

They sat down to have coffee and eat a traditional Filipino breakfast called Pandesal (Bread of Salt) along with scrambled egg and a slice of cheese, Ernie and Andre were eating and dipping the Pandesal in the hot coffee. Cora and Danilo were dipping their Pandesal in the 'chocolate' made from 'tableya' (pure cocoa). Then, there was a brief silence. By saying nothing, they all were sharing the same story and concern.

After breakfast, "Let's see how the weather looks in the late afternoon, I believe it will clear up by night and we will be able to go there tomorrow morning," Ernie said.

"I understand…I am eager to go to the colony," Andre responded, looking out through the window mournfully at the pouring rain.

Afterward, he stood up and then said, "Thank you, dear friend, I will see you tomorrow in the early morning." He grabbed his rain jacket, waved to all, and left to go back to his home. This time, walking under heavy rain did not bother him a bit, his mind was somewhere else. When arriving home, his family had no question as to why he came home alone and why he was soaking wet. Andre changed his wet clothes and sat down quietly the whole day. And then in the early evening, there was silence outside, and it stopped raining.

On the next day, Danilo and his father got up early around five to get ready for the big day. As luck would have it, there wasn't a cloud in the sky, and Andre was outside knocking at the door.

Upon opening the door, "Good morning, friends...Please do not bother preparing breakfast, I got food and water for all of us. I also got extra food for Carlo," Andre said while his eyes filled with tears.

"Okay...Let's go. It seems like today will be a good day to sail," Ernie said and three were on their way rushing to the boat.

When arriving at the boat, the sun was brightly rising above the sea and appears welcoming of the new day. Its golden disc seems to be rising and rising and the sea birds were singing to its shine. The day looks beautiful so far!

"The sea looks calm and I think we should be on the colony's shore in about two hours or so," said Ernie. "Let's keep our fingers crossed." Danilo and Andre nodded. Then after almost two hours, the trio just arrived and were on their way to the colony through the mangroves. Walking today was more difficult as the water was everywhere. The creek beds held water, which made it difficult to swing across as the water was rushing down. Walking through to get to the colony this time was a little scary.

Finally, they were on the colony's outskirts, this time, it took them almost an hour to get there. Upon arrival, "Daddy! Danilo! Daddy! Danilo!" Carlo was screaming and rushing toward them. He was in desperation and fear. Quickly, he was as fast as his scream could reach them. He hugged his dad, Danilo, and then Ernie and cried as he was sobbing without restraint.

"It was a nightmare, Dad...I do not know what happened to me. I was dreaming then I got up to find myself here with the monkeys," sorrowful Carlo said.

Then, "Why did you leave me here?" he asked Danilo.

"I had a bad dream about you, you became a tarsier. Um...Um...Um...Am confused!"

"I will explain to you later when we leave here...Be patient for now," Danilo stated as Carlo's dad was sobbing while hugging and sniffing his son.

"I got you some food," his dad gave him a sandwich and an apple.

"I am so hungry, I want to see Mom, my siblings, and Grandpa and Grandma," he said while eating the sandwich.

In the meantime, Mother Monkey and her family became very emotional. Mother Monkey was shedding tears, she could barely conceal her delight. At this moment, Carlo got down on his knees, whimpering a cry for forgiveness from his dad, and begging his dad to take him home. His dad, Danilo, and Ernie were all crying with joy. His dad reacted by saying, "It is the best day of my life!" his tears of happiness were pouring all down his face. Quickly, all turn toward Mother Monkey and bowed to her expressing their appreciation. Then they hugged her, hugged all monkeys, waved goodbye, and then left the colony. It was the happiest moment for all!

When arrived at the boat, Danilo started telling Carlo the long story of their disappearance and what had happened from the moment they entered the Hills till the moment they arrived at the colony to pick him up. Carlo was in complete shock, and fear, and pressing his palms to his face. His imagination took him too far! Danilo was more relaxed. He had so much to tell tearful Carlo.

"I am so sad and feel bad that we blew off last school term," Carlo was telling Danilo. "Oh…Me too, I feel bad. I've never skipped a class in my life. I don't even imagine that I will ever miss a future class," Danilo responded.

They sat in the boat, staring at each other quietly. Their blood was pounding in their temple.

They both felt the beginnings of a massive future change.

"We are going to be serious and outstanding students," said Danilo.

"And we are going to be excellent, disciplined, and loyal kids that our parents will be proud of. Additionally, we will work on holidays to help our parents," added Carlo.

"And yet, it is also my firm belief," Danilo replied, "that we should help our family too."

"One more thing," Danilo added, "We should also be advocates and educators on conservation education. We must enhance the public's understanding of wildlife and the need to conserve the places animals live. We must educate fishers about marine animals so that they may come to appreciate them and protect their fragile marine habitats and avoid hurting them."

Carlo shrieked in excitement and said, "Let's do it! Let's do it! Besides our family, animals helped us survive!"

"I think some of the tarsiers in the Hills were kids like us, we will need to do something to help them too. We could've still been tarsiers if it wasn't for the Mother Monkey who accidentally met us the night before we arrived at the Hills," Carlo added and cried as he reflected on their lucky encounter with the Mother Monkey.

"It is okay, Son! No need to worry anymore, we all love you, and are happy you are back," his dad said. "I am so happy today. Again, this is my happiest day ever! Your mom will be very happy as soon as she sees you." His dad's tears overflowed with joy and fell just like the rushing creek water that had just passed by the colony.

That day, sailing back to Calape was pleasant and the waters of the Bohol Sea were blue and calm. They did not have to tackle rough waves, it seems as if Mother Nature wants to add more color to their happiness. At that time, Ernie was holding firmly onto the steering wheel, he was wiping his eyes. That seemed to be a happy and unforgettable time for everyone. Then, "Hey, guys! Please remember that there aren't chocolates in the Hills!" Ernie said with a big smile to conceal his tears.

Everyone laughed, and Ernie responded by saying, "Agreed! You took the words right out of my mouth. We're in accord!" Ernie replied with his usual happy smile. Both Danilo and Carlo reciprocated with a forced smile, they were trying to hide their uncomfortable feeling regarding their unpleasant adventure.

"We would never do anything stupid like what we did," Danilo said. Then he grinned at everyone and hugged Carlo. Their happy reunion trip went so fast and in less than two hours, Ernie docked his boat by the shore of Calape. Everyone enjoyed every single minute of the boat ride. It was wonderful. The memory still mesmerizes them.

All of a sudden, "Can we stop for a minute at the Banana Shore and see if Paco is there?" asked Danilo.

"Let's do so quickly as we need to get to Carlo's family home, they are desperately waiting for news," Ernie responded and all walked fast to the quiet Banana Shore, yet Paco was not there. "Let's take the Jeepney to get home faster, *kapatid na lalaki* (a phrase that here means 'Brother')," suggested Andre.

"I agree, *kapatid na lalaki*, let's move quickly," responded Ernie then all walked toward the nearby *Jeepney*.

In less than twenty minutes, they arrived home to an unusual heroes' welcome. Everyone in the neighborhood ran to greet them and hugged the boys, neighbors were bursting into tears. As you got closer to their home, his mom came out and jumped to her feet. "Carlo!" she screamed and held her son tight. Carlo's grandparents, siblings, and neighbors were screaming in happiness. Flanked by lots of people, Carlo and Danilo were tearful, they sobbed. The news spread fast, and in a matter of a few minutes, the house was crowded with wish-wishers. Cora, Friends, and neighbors' alike brought food and sweets in celebration, they can now celebrate the safe return of the two boys. Outside the house, kids were sitting on the sidewalk talking about their return and waiting their turn to see Danilo and Carlo.

It was Friday evening and people continued flooding into the house, many asking how it happened, and some saying what they had been told. It was interesting when a neighbor whispered, "So it wasn't true that both kids were swallowed by a dolphin!" Some looked funny at her and others smiled.

Suddenly, another neighbor just came in. Dressed in faded blue jeans and a blue undershirt. She had sneakers on her feet but no socks and was carrying her infant baby in her left arm. This woman went straight to Carlo and gave him a big hug. She was eager to talk. She sighed and then spoke in a high tone, "Um! There's a rumor going around the neighborhood that a big monkey kidnapped the boys, is it a true story?" Some people reacted by smiling while others quietly laughed. And then one lady stared glumly at those who talked, then smirked, and said, "Shhh…I beg your pardon! It is over and the boys are back safe; let's stop asking how and why or suggesting stories. Unless they tell us what we need to know, let's respect their privacy. The good news, is the kids are back safe!"

While other people nodded their heads, others gave the lady thumbs up. Later on, Mr. Adrian, the principal of the school dropped by to show his support to the family and the boys after learning that Danilo and Carlo were back. He hugged them tight and expressed his and other teachers' willingness to help them.

"We are happy that you are back safe," Mr. Adrian said in a low voice. "The teachers and kids at school would treat you with respect. You wouldn't have to talk to anybody if you don't want to." His eyes filled up with tears.

"I am sorry, sir!" Danilo's voice broke.

Carlo nodded, looked at the floor, and repeated in his low voice the exact words that Danilo just said, "I am sorry, sir!" His mom held him closely as others can hear him crying. Mr. Adrian put his arm around the boys and said, "All the teachers would be especially nice to you. They miss both of you and they all love you!"

People stayed late during the celebration. Danilo and Carlo's families sobbed tears of joy.

Their mothers' eyes were welled with tears, and their lips formed a smile. This day was very different, many people cried because they were happy.

Danilo and Carlo were in a serious urge to see Paco and spend the weekend with him before starting school on Monday. They did not sleep well, they were happy that the nightmare is over, but still thinking about their unforgettable adventure.

On the next day, Carlo arrived early and knocked on the door. He didn't need to wait long; Danilo was ready to go. They were racing to the closest *Jeepney's* location to get there, they jumped inside, and sat down on the *Jeepney* staring at people walking and crossing the roads from all directions. They were happily watching street vendors cooking and selling various local foods on the side of the street. They were smiling as they were watching people buying various items such as onion, garlic, dried fish, pepper, tomatoes, banana, mango, pineapple, spices, and other fruits and vegetables on vendor stalls.

In less than twenty minutes, they got to the Banana shore. Carlo ran toward the water, started kicking seawater up into Danilo's face, and splashing everywhere. He felt a surge of happiness. Danilo splashed back and then pushed Carlo into the water, he could hardly contain his happiness at seeing and playing again with his friend.

"Paco should be here anytime soon!" said Danilo. "I can't wait to see him and hug him!" replied Carlo.

As they were swimming and playing while waiting for Paco, Danilo stood up and said, "Let's have fun…Let's sing a new song that I wrote last night. It is called, no chocolates on the Hill!"

"You must be kidding!" Carlo's spirits were flying high.

"Why not? Repeat after me," Danilo asked Carlo.

No chocolates on the Hills…Tell who you like to tell

I'd rather go to school…Instead of being a fool

I'd sit and read my book…And wait for the school's bell

No chocolates on the Hills…Tell who you like to tell

****

When arriving there…I wasted in despair
Surrounded by tarsiers…I was driven with fear!
And wished I was a bear! And wished I was a bear!
No chocolates and no mango! No coconuts dancing the tango!
Not even a tiny pear! Not even a tiny pear!
No chocolates…No chocolates…No chocolates on the Hills!

"Ha…Ha…Ha! This is brilliant, hilarious, and a fantastic song! I did not know you got the talent to do so," Carlo said.

Danilo laughed and showed him a big smile. "I knew you'd appreciate it…This song is only for us and not for anyone else!"

"Agreed!" Carlo responded.

In a couple of minutes, they burst into laughter as they sang, *No chocolates on the Hills.*

Seemed as if the sunshine flooded their soul and their hopes soared as they waited to meet Paco. Danilo and Carlo continued playing and swimming while waiting for Paco, but he did not show up this time.

"I am so scared, I hope he is okay," a distressed Danilo said.

"Do not worry, my friend, I think he is confused with time. We will come back tomorrow. Now let's go home, we don't want our family to worry anymore," said Carlo and sadly they went home without seeing Paco.

The same thing happened on Sunday, they waited and waited but Paco did not show up. No one knows what happened to Paco! Only time will tell whether he is still alive or not.

If alive, will he ever come back to the shore? What might happen if he does not come? Additionally, time will tell whether Danilo and Carlo will do something to help make the Hills peaceful and free from the Evil Giant. Fighting the Evil Giant, how possible it is and how will it be done? Danilo and Carlo will be searching for the light at the end of the tunnel; the moment of pause shown here conveys need, and longing, but also relief, or even hope.

It seems that every pain or challenge gives us a lesson and every lesson change our life...Don't give up!

www.ingramcontent.com/pod-product-compliance
Lightning Source LLC
Chambersburg PA
CBHW052052150726

48002CB00002B/863